The Bishop's Apron

A study in the origins of a great family

W. Somerset Maugham

The Bishop's Apron: A study in the origins of a great family

ISBN: 978-1-61895-978-2

CONTENTS

I

THE world takes people very willingly at the estimate in which they hold themselves. With a fashionable bias for expression in a foreign tongue it calls modesty mauvaise honte; and the impudent are thought merely to have a proper opinion of their merit. But Ponsonby was really an imposing personage. His movements were measured and noiseless; and he wore the sombre garb of a gentleman's butler with impressive dignity. He was a large man, flabby and corpulent, with a loose, smooth skin. His face, undisturbed by the rapid play of expression, which he would have thought indecorous, had a look of placid respectability; his eyes, with their puffy lower lids, rested on surrounding objects heavily; and his earnest, obsequious voice gave an impression of such overwhelming piety that your glance, involuntarily, fell to his rotund calves for the gaiters episcopal.

He looked gravely at the table set out for luncheon, while Alfred, the footman, walked round it, placing bread in each napkin.

"Is Tommy Tiddler coming to-day, Mr. Ponsonby?" he asked.

"His lordship is expected," returned the butler, with a frigid stare.

He emphasised the aspirate to mark his disapproval of the flippancy wherewith his colleague referred to a person who was not only the brother of his master, but a member of the aristocracy.

"Here he is!" said Alfred, unabashed, looking out of the window. "He's just drove up in a cab."

Lord Spratte walked up the steps and rang the bell. Though Ponsonby had seen him two or three times a week for ten years, he gave no sign of recognition.

"Am I expected to luncheon to-day, Ponsonby?"

"Yes, my lord."

Lord Spratte was middle-aged, of fresh complexion notwithstanding his grey hair; and his manner was quick and breezy. He carried his years and the increasing girth which accompanied them, with a graceful light-heartedness; and was apt to flatter himself that with the light behind he might still pass for five-and-thirty. He had neither the wish nor the intention to grow old. But the man of fifty, seeking to make the most of himself, must use many careful adjustments. Not for him are the loose, ill-fitting clothes that become a stripling of eighteen; his tailor needs a world of skill to counteract the slackening of muscle and to minimize the excess of avoirdupois. On his toilet-table are numerous pots and jars and bottles, and each is a device to persuade himself that the troublesome years are not marching on. He takes more care of his hands than a professional beauty. Above all, his hair is a source of anxiety. Lord Spratte by many experiments had learnt exactly how to dress it so that no unbecoming baldness was displayed; but he never seized a brush and comb without thinking, like Achilles stalking melancholy through the fields of death, that he would much sooner be a crossing-sweeper of fifteen than a peer of the realm at fifty.

"Do you insist on leading me upstairs like a ewe-lamb, Ponsonby?" he asked.

The butler's face outlined the merest shadow of a smile as, silently, he preceded Lord Spratte to the drawing-room. For nothing in the world would he have omitted the customary ceremonies of polite society.

"Lord Spratte," he announced.

The guest advanced and saw his sister Sophia, his brother Theodore, his nephew and his niece. Lady Sophia, a handsome and self-assured woman of five-and-fifty, the eldest of the family, put aside her book and rose to kiss him. Canon Spratte extended two fingers.

"Good heavens, have you invited me to a family party!"

"Than which, I venture to think, there can be nothing more charming, nothing more beautiful, and nothing more entertaining," replied the Canon, gaily.

"Theodore is cultivating domesticity," retorted the peer, with a look at his younger brother. "I believe he wants to be made a bishop."

"You take nothing seriously, Thomas. It is a failing of which I cannot but recommend you to correct yourself."

"Stow it, Theodore," replied the other, unmoved.

Theodore Spratte, Vicar of St. Gregory's, South Kensington, and Canon of Tercanbury, was the youngest son of the first Earl Spratte, Lord Chancellor of England. He was a handsome man, tall and erect; and his presence was commanding. His comely looks had been to him through life a source of abiding pleasure. He preserved the slenderness, the brisk carriage of youth; and though but little younger than his brother, his fair hair, turning now to grey, remained profuse and curling. His fine blue eyes looked out upon the world with a happy self-confidence, and his mobile, shapely mouth was ever ready to break into a smile. The heartiness of his laughter sufficed to make all and sundry his particular friends. It was pleasant to meet a man who was so clean and fresh, always so admirably dressed, and whose appearance was so prepossessing. But he was nowhere more imposing than in the pulpit; for he wore his cassock and surplice, his scarlet hood, with a reassuring dash which convinced you that here was a pilot in whom you need not hesitate to set your trust. He had a certain gift for oratory. His voice was resonant and well modulated. The charm of his active personality was such that though, in those flowing periods and that wealth of metaphor, amid these sounding, forcible adjectives, the matter of his discourse often escaped you, you felt notwithstanding exhilarated and content. If his sermons redounded to his own honour rather than to the honour of God, it was not Canon Spratte who suffered.

When he was left a widower with two young children, his sister Sophia, who had remained unmarried, came to live with him. In course of time Lionel, his son, grew up, entered the Church, and became his curate. His daughter Winnie was twenty-one, and in her fragile, delicate way as pretty as a shepherdess of Dresden china. She had all the charm of innocence, and such knowledge of the world as three seasons in London and the daily example of her father could give her.

"By the way, Lionel, I suppose you took that wedding at 2.30 yesterday?"

"Yes," answered the curate.

But the curtness of his reply was almost injurious contrasted with his father's florid delivery; it seemed barely decent to treat in monosyllables with the Vicar of St. Gregory's. His lightest observations were coloured by that rich baritone so that they gained a power and a significance which other men, less happily gifted, have only in treating of grave affairs.

"I often wonder it's worth your while to marry quite poor people," suggested Lord Spratte. "Why don't you send them down to the East End?"

"Our duty, my dear Thomas, we have to do our duty," replied Canon Spratte.

Ponsonby, entering the room to intimate that luncheon was ready, looked significantly at Lady Sophia, without speaking, and silently withdrew.

"I see that the Bishop of Barchester is dangerously ill," said Lionel, when they were seated.

Lionel was as tall and fair as his father, but lacked his energy and his force of character. He was dressed as little like a clergyman as possible.

"I'm told he's dying," answered the Canon, gravely. "He's been out of health for a long time, and I cannot help thinking that when the end comes it will be a happy release."

"I met him once and thought him a very brilliant man," remarked Lady Sophia.

"Andover?" cried the Canon, with surprise, throwing himself back in his chair. "My dear Sophia! I know he had a certain reputation for learning, but I never had any great opinion of it."

Lady Sophia for all reply pursed her lips. She exchanged a glance with Lord Spratte.

"Of course I am the last person to say anything against a man who stands on the threshold of eternity," added the Canon. "But between ourselves, if the truth must be told—he was nothing more than a doddering old idiot. And a man of no family."

Than this, in Theodore Spratte's judgment, nothing could be said more utterly disparaging.

"I wonder who'll succeed him," said Lionel, thoughtfully.

"I really don't know who there is with any great claim upon the Government." He met his brother's bantering smile, and quick to catch its meaning, answered without hesitation. "To tell you the truth, Thomas, I shouldn't be at all surprised if Lord Stonehenge offered the bishopric to me."

"You'd look rather a toff in leggings," observed the other. "Wouldn't he, Sophia?"

Lady Sophia gave the Canon an inquiring stare.

"My dear Tommy, I've not seen his legs for forty years."

"I think this is hardly a matter upon which you should exercise your humour, my dear," retorted the Canon, with a twinkle in his eye.

"Well, I hope you will accept no bishopric until you've made quite sure that the golf-links are beyond reproach," said Lord Spratte.

"I'll tell Lord Stonehenge that an eighteen-hole course is a sine qua non of my elevation to the Episcopacy," retorted the Canon, ironically.

Between Lord Spratte and his sister on the one hand and Theodore on the other, was an unceasing duel, in which the parson fought for the respect due to his place and dignity, while the others were determined to suffer no nonsense. They attacked his pretension with flouting and battered his pomposity with ridicule. To anything in the nature of rhodomontade they were merciless, and in their presence he found it needful to observe a certain measure. He knew that no society was august enough to abash them into silence, and so took care not to expose himself under very public circumstances to the irony of the one or to the brutal mocking of the other. But the struggle was not altogether unpleasant. He could hit back with a good deal of vigour, and never hesitated to make plain statements in plain language. His position gave him the advantage that he could marshal on his side the forces of morality and religion; and when they had dealt so good a blow that he could not conceal his discomfiture, he was able to regain his self-esteem by calling them blasphemous or vulgar.

The Canon turned to his daughter with an affectionate smile.

"And what have you been doing this morning, Winnie?"

"I went to see the model dwellings that Mr. Railing is interested in."

"By Jove, you're not goin' in for district visitin', Winnie?" cried her uncle, putting up his eye-glass. "I hope you won't catch anything."

Winnie blushed a little under his stare.

"The condition of the poor is awfully bad. I think one ought to do something."

"Who is Mr. Railing?" inquired Lionel. "One of the Worcestershire Railings?"

"No, just a common or garden Railing," said the Canon.

He rubbed his hands and looked round the table for appreciation of this mild jest, but only his curate was civil enough to smile.

"He's a mighty clever young man, and I think he'll be very useful to me," he added.

"I notice that your actions are always governed by unselfish motives," murmured Lady Sophia.

"God helps those who help themselves. Mr. Railing is a Christian Socialist and writes for the Radical papers. I think he has a future, and I feel it my duty to give him some encouragement." His voice assumed those rolling, grandiloquent tones which rang so effectively in St. Gregory's Church. "Now-a-days, when Socialism is rapidly becoming a power in the land, when it is spreading branches into every stratum of society, it behoves us to rally it to the Church. Christianity is Socialism."

Lady Sophia gave a deprecating smile: "My dear Theodore, remember that only your family is present."

But it was not easy to stem the flood of Canon Spratte's eloquence. He threw back his handsome head and looked at the full-length portrait of his father, in robes of office, which adorned the wall.

"I pride myself above all things upon being abreast of the times. Every movement that savours of advance will find in me an enthusiastic supporter. My father, the late Lord Chancellor, was one of the first to perceive the coming strength of the people. And I am proud to know that my family has always identified itself with the future. Advance," again the thrilling voice rang out. "Advance has always been our watchword, advance and progress."

Lord Spratte gave a low chuckle, for his brother was delivered into his hand.

"You speak as if we'd come over with the Conquest, Theodore."

Canon Spratte turned to him coolly.

"Have you never looked out the name of Spratte in Debrett?"

"Frequently. I find the peerage excellent readin' to fall back on when there's nothin' in the sportin' papers. But it's no bloomin' good, Theodore; the family tree's all bogus. A man with the name of Spratte didn't have ancestors at the battle of Hastings."

"I wish to goodness you would express yourself in grammatical English," answered the Canon, irritably. "I detest slang, and I deplore this habit of yours of omitting the terminal letter of certain words."

"You digress, my dear Theodore."

"Not at all! I don't deny that the family has had its vicissitudes; you will find it difficult to discover one in the peerage that has not. At all events my father implicitly believed in the family tree."

"Well, he must have been a pretty innocent old buffer to do that. I never found any one else who would. Upon my word, I don't see why a man called Spratte should have ancestors called Montmorency."

"I should have thought that even in your brief stay at Oxford you learnt enough natural history to know that every man must have a father," retorted the Canon, ironically.

Lord Spratte had been sent down from the 'Varsity for some escapade of his early youth, and for thirty years his brother had never hesitated to remind him of it.

"All I can say is that if a man called Spratte had a father called Montmorency, the less said about it the better," he answered. "I may be particular, but it don't sound moral to me."

"Your facetiousness is misplaced, Thomas, and considering

that Winnie is present, the taste of it is more than doubtful. The connection at which you are pleased to sneer is perfectly clear and perfectly honourable. In 1631, Aubrey de Montmorency married...."

But Lady Sophia, in tones of entreaty, interrupted: "Oh, Theodore, Theodore, not again!"

He gave her a glance of some vexation, but held his tongue.

"The first millionaire I meet who's lookin' out for a family tree, I'll sell him mine for fifty quid," said Lord Spratte. "And I'm blowed if it wouldn't be cheap at the price, considerin' that it's chock full of Howards and Talbots and de Veres—to say nothin' of a whole string of Montmorencys."

"You don't know Sir John Durant, the brewer, do you, father?" asked Lionel. "He told me that since they gave him a baronetcy people have been regularly sending him a new and original family tree once a week."

"He must have quite a forest by now," answered Lord Spratte. "What does he use 'em for—hop-poles?"

"I should have thought they would make admirable Christmas presents for his poor relations," suggested the Canon, who could not resist his little joke even on subjects dear to him. He turned again to his daughter. "By the way, Winnie, I find I shall be unable to go to Mr. Railing's meeting to-morrow."

"He'll be awfully disappointed. He was expecting you to make a speech."

"I've promised Lady Vizard to lunch with her to meet the Princess of Wartburg-Hochstein. I shouldn't be able to get away early enough. A clergyman's time is really never his own, and the Princess wishes particularly to meet me."

"People so often forget that even Royal Personages have spiritual difficulties," murmured Lady Sophia.

"I shall write a little note to Mr. Railing wishing him luck, and with your permission, Sophia, I'll ask him to tea afterwards."

"Is he presentable?"

"He's a gentleman, Aunt Sophia," cried Winnie. "And he's as beautiful as a Greek god."

Winnie flushed as she said this, and dropped her eyes. They were pleasant and blue like her father's, but instead of his bold friendliness had a plaintiveness of expression which was rather charming. They seemed to appeal for confidence and for affection.

"Shall I come and address your meeting, Winnie?" asked Lord Spratte, amused at her enthusiasm. "What is it about?"

"Teetotalism!" she smiled.

"Most of the London clergy go in for that now, don't they?"

remarked Lionel. “The bishop asked me the other day whether I was an abstainer.”

“The bishop is a man of no family, Lionel,” retorted his father. “Personally I make no secret of the fact that I do not approve of teetotalism. Temperance, yes! But how can you be temperate if you abstain entirely? Corn and wine, the wheat, the barley, the vine, are ubiquitous; the corn strengthens, the wine gladdens man’s heart, as at the marriage feast in Cana of Galilee.”

Lord Spratte opened his mouth to speak.

“I wish you wouldn’t continually interrupt me, Thomas,” cried the Canon, before his brother could utter a word. “He who has solemnly pledged himself to total abstinence has surrendered to a society of human and modern institution his liberty to choose. Now what is it you wished to say, Thomas?”

“I merely wanted to ask Ponsonby for more potatoes.”

“I knew it was some flippant observation,” retorted the Canon.

“The bishop suggested that total abstinence in the clergy served as an example,” said Lionel, mildly.

“As an example it has been a dismal failure. For many years I have searched for some successful results, for one man who would prove to me that, being a drunkard, he was so much impressed by the example of his clergyman, who for his sake and imitation ceased to drink his glass of beer at luncheon, his glass of port at dinner, or his glass of whisky and water at night, that he broke away from his vicious indulgence and became a sober man.”

Ponsonby stood at the Canon’s elbow, patiently waiting for the end of this harangue.

“Hock, sir?” said he, in sepulchral tones.

“Certainly, Ponsonby, certainly!” replied the Canon, so vigorously that the butler was not a little disconcerted. “What do you think of this hock, Thomas? Not bad, I flatter myself.”

He raised the glass to his nose and inhaled the pleasant odour. He drank his wine and smiled. An expression of placid satisfaction came over his face. He favoured the company with a Latin quotation:

> *“O quam bonum est,*
> *O quam jucundum est,*
> *Poculis fraternis gaudere.”*

II

IT was one of Canon Spratte's peculiarities that he liked to read his Times before any other member of his family. He found a peculiar delight in opening it himself, and likened the perusal of a newspaper which some one else had read, to the drinking of milk from which a dishonest dairyman had skimmed the cream. Next morning, running his eye down the list of contents, he discovered that the Bishop of Barchester was dead.

"Poor Andover is no more, Sophia," he remarked, with a decent solemnity.

He ate his kidney absently, and it was not till he passed his coffee-cup to Lady Sophia to be refilled that he made any observation.

"It's really almost providential that the poor old man should depart this life on the very day I am to meet Lord Stonehenge at dinner. I'd better have the pair to-night, Sophia."

"Where are you dining?"

"At the Hollingtons," he answered. "Last time a bishopric was vacant, the Prime Minister practically assured me that I should have the next."

"He's probably done the same to half the school-masters in England."

"Nonsense! Who is there that could take it? They've none of them half the claims that I have."

Theodore Spratte never concealed from the world that he rated himself highly. He esteemed bashfulness a sign of bad manners, and was used to say that a man who pretended not to know his own value was a possing fool.

"It's a ridiculous system altogether to give a bishopric to Tom Noddy because he's taught Latin verses to a parcel of stupid school-boys. And besides, as the youngest son of the late Lord Chancellor, I think I may expect something from my country."

"Pray pass me the toast," said Lady Sophia.

"I'm not a vain man, but I honestly think I have the right to some recognition. As my father, the late Lord Chancellor of England, often said...."

"I wish to goodness you wouldn't talk of him as if he were your father only, Theodore," interrupted Lady Sophia, not without irritation. "I have just as much right to him as you."

"I think you asked for the toast, my dear."

Presently Canon Spratte, taking the paper with him, retired to his study. He was a man of regular habits, knowing that to acquire such is the first step to greatness, episcopal and otherwise; and after breakfast he was used to smoke his pipe, meditate, and read the Times. But this morning, somewhat agitated by the news of Bishop Andover's demise, he took from the shelves that book which at present was his only contribution to the great literature of England. On the death of his father, laden with years and with honours, Canon Spratte had begun immediately to gather materials for a biography. This was eventually published under the title: Life and Letters of Josiah Spratte, Lord Chancellor of England. It was in two volumes, magnificently bound in calf, with the family arms, a blaze of gold, on the side.

When the Canon set about this great work he went to his sister and begged her to make notes of her recollections.

"You can help me a great deal, Sophia," he said. "With your woman's intelligence, you will have noticed a good many points which have escaped me. The masculine intellect takes in the important main lines, whereas women observe only the frivolous details. But I recognize that it is just these frivolous details, properly sorted, which will give life and variety to that grand career absorbed by affairs of State and the advantage of the nation."

Lady Sophia, accustomed to these tirades, smiled dryly and said: "Shall I tell you the very first thing I remember, Theodore? I can't have been more than six years old, but I have never forgotten it."

"That is very interesting. Let me put it down at once."

He took from his pocket the little book, which he carried with him always to jot down the thoughts that periodically occurred to him.

"Now, Sophia."

"Father and mother were having a conversation, and suddenly father beat his fist on the table so that the whole room shook."

"Yes, he had that energetic, effective way of expressing himself," said the Canon. "He was a man of really forceful character. That is a point upon which I mean to lay great stress."

"He beat his fist on the table and he roared out at the top of his voice: 'Your father's a damned fool, Maria; and your mother's a damned fool, Maria; but, by gad, you're a bigger damned fool than both of them put together.' "

The Canon sprang up and throwing back his head with a gesture habitual to him, drew to his full, imposing height.

"You shock and surprise me, Sophia. If these are your recollections, I advise you to forget them as quickly as you possibly can."

Nor had he better success with his brother.

"I wonder whether you can give me no anecdotes, no interesting side-lights on our father's character? I am determined to make my biography as complete as possible."

"I'll give you an anecdote by all means," said Lord Spratte. "You remember that the old 'un very much objected to potatoes baked in their skins."

"A very pardonable and interesting idiosyncrasy of genius," interposed the biographer.

"Well, one Sunday night when we had people to supper, by some accident they were brought in. The servant handed the dish to father. Father looked at him and slowly rose to his feet. 'Don't you know, you idiot,' he bellowed, 'that I don't like potatoes baked in their skins?' He took them out of the dish, one by one, while the servant stood petrified, and threw them with all his might at the pictures on the walls. Each picture had its potato till the dish was empty. Then he sat down again calmly and began to eat his supper."

"I shall certainly put down nothing in my biography which tends to cast ridicule or odium on the memory of a great man," said Canon Spratte, frigidly. "My motto is: De mortuis nil nisi bonum."

On this principle the Life and Letters was written. To testify to filial admiration there were in St. Gregory's Vicarage no less than three portraits of the first Earl Spratte, but the most characteristic was a copy of that which the Chancellor himself, with due regard to his fame and importance, had bequeathed to the National Portrait Gallery. It showed the great man seated, his hands grasping the arms of his chair with the savage vigour that was customary with him. They were strong, large hands, and the tendons stood out from the brutal force wherewith he held them. He looked the spectator full in the face, sitting very squarely, bent forward in the despotic attitude which all who had appeared before him knew so well. He wore the full-bottomed wig of his office and the gorgeous robes, edged with gold. His head was thrust out and he stared from under his shaggy brows with an expression of ruthless violence; his strong features were set in a villainous scowl; his hard, cruel mouth was clenched as though he were determined that nothing should affect his will. And the idea which the fine portrait gave, was borne out by the memoirs of the time.

Springing, notwithstanding the Canon's grandiloquence, from the dregs of commercial life, Josiah Spratte had fought his way to the greatest prize of his calling by an indomitable will and a truculent savagery that spared neither enemies nor friends. Though endowed by nature with no great subtlety of mind, he had a gift of fluent speech, an imperturbable self-confidence, and a physique of extraordinary vigour. He was unhampered by any thought for the susceptibilities of others, and he was regardless of good manners. He bullied his way to the Woolsack by the weight of his personality and the harsh roar of his voice. From the outset of his career, as a junior, he treated his leaders with unhidden contempt. He used the solicitors who gave him briefs like vermin, dealing with them as might a harsh master with a set of ignorant and rebellious schoolboys. They hated him, but were impressed withal, and quickly brought him more work than he could do. Then, beginning to feel his power, he browbeat the court so that weak judges were like wax in his hands and juries trembled at his ferocious glance. He went into Parliament and trampled impartially upon his associates and his opponents. He excited more hatred than any one of his generation, for he was insolent, overbearing, and impatient of contradiction; but in a short while the Government was forced to make him Attorney-General. From the beginning his mind had been set on the ultimate goal, and he waited till the Chancellor of that time died. This was the most critical point of his life, for all concerned understood perfectly at what Josiah Spratte aimed; but now all the bitterness, anger, and loathing he had so wilfully aroused, were banded against him; and he had to fight as well against the rivalry of some and the bitterness of others. But like a lion at bay, with magnificent self-confidence, he squared himself to bear down all obstacles. The Government was undecided. A certain eminent lawyer, Sir Robert Parkleigh, had claims upon it which were undeniable. Having held office in a previous administration he had waived his right to promotion on the understanding that his reward should be great thereafter: he was a man of vigorous understanding, learned, urbane and of great family. The appointment would be very popular. But the Attorney-General was not a man to be trifled with, and a go-between was sent unofficially to learn his views.

"I suppose Parkleigh will get the Chancellorship," said this person, in the course of an amiable conversation.

"You suppose nothing of the sort," shouted Josiah Spratte. His face grew red with passion and his scowl deepened as the veins of his forehead stood out like knotted cords. He fixed on the man those piercing eyes which seemed to read into the soul, discovering shameful secrets. "You've been sent to find out what I thought about the Chancellorship? It's what I suspected. Don't deny it!"

Beads of sweat stood on the other's brow as the Attorney-General towered over him, threatening and peremptory. He vowed he had received no such mission.

"Don't deny it, I tell you," cried Josiah Spratte. Then, furiously, he walked up and down the room. "Tell them," he hissed at length, with undescribable venom, "Tell them that if Parkleigh is made Chancellor, I'll kick the Government out. By God, they shan't stay in a month!"

While the appointment was pending, a great lady, suffering under some brutal affront, sought to beard the lion.

"Do you know what people are saying about you, Mr. Attorney? They're wondering who this sprat is that we are asked to swallow."

Sir Josiah looked at her.

"Tell your friends, Madam, to be thankful the sprat is not a whale, because even if he were, by God they'd have to swallow him. And what's more, they'd have to pretend they liked him!"

Shortly afterwards the Prime Minister wrote a very civil note to his subordinate offering him the much-coveted place. Josiah Spratte was raised to the Peerage. A second term of office was rewarded by new honour, and he became Earl Spratte of Beachcombe and Viscount Rallington.

But the great lawyer carried also into private life the tones with which he cowed juries and sent witnesses fainting from the box. He never spoke but to command and gave no order without a string of oaths. When he fell into a temper, which happened several times a day, he could be heard from top to bottom of the house. His wife, his servants, trembled before him; his children in his presence spoke in whispers, and he took pleasure in humiliating them with brutal raillery. He met his match but twice. The first time was at his club when he was playing whist. This was his favourite relaxation, and he was always to be found in the card-room about six o'clock waiting for a rubber. One day by chance a fourth could not be found, and the Chancellor himself went into the smoking-room to look for a player. It was a sunny afternoon in July, and the place was deserted, except for a young guardsman who sat comfortably sleeping in an arm-chair. Without hesitation Lord Spratte shook him violently till he was wide awake, and asked if he knew the game. He answered that he played very badly and would much sooner resume his nap; but Lord Spratte declined to hear excuses, and dragged him by sheer force into the card-room. The soldier had only spoken the truth when he described himself as a bad player, and since he was the Chancellor's partner, things did not go very smoothly. The elder man took no trouble to hide his annoyance when the other made a mistake, and expressed his opinion of the subaltern's intelligence with more bluntness than civility.

"Oh, confound you, shut up!" cried the guardsman at last. "How d'you expect a fellow to play if you go on ragging him like a fish-wife?"

"I don't think you know who I am, sir," answered the Chancellor, with frowning brows.

"Oh yes, I do! You're the Lord Chancellor, aren't you? But you might mind your manners for all that. You're not in your dirty police-court now."

For the rest of that rubber the distinguished lawyer never opened his mouth.

But next time he was worsted in debate the results were more serious. Lord Spratte, still restless after the attainment of his ambition, was seized with the desire to found a great family; and on this account wished his eldest son, who had assumed the title of Viscount Rallington, to marry a certain heiress of important connections. The lady was not unwilling, but Rallington stubbornly refused. At first, white with rage, Lord Spratte asked how he dared to cross him; and he showered upon his son that abundant vituperation of which he was the finest master in England. But without effect. The Chancellor was so astounded at this display of spirit that for once in his life he condescended to argue. His son stood firm. Then the old man burst out again with violent temper.

"And who the devil are you?" he cried. "Haven't I raised you from the gutter? What would you be without me? By God, you shall do whatever I tell you."

Rallington lost all patience. He put off the timidity with which for years he had endured so much and went up to his father.

"Look here, don't talk to me like that. I'll marry a barmaid if I choose, and be damned to you!"

The Chancellor's hair stood on end with wrath, and he gasped for breath. His passion was such that for a minute he could not speak. Then his son, driven at length to open rebellion, poured out the hatred which had so long accumulated. He reminded him of the tyranny with which he had used his whole family, and the terror in which he had held them. He had robbed them of all freedom, so that they were slaves to his every whim. To his angry violence and to his selfishness all their happiness had been sacrificed.

"You've been a bullying ruffian all your life, and no one has had the pluck to stand up to you. I'm sick of it, and I won't stand it any more. D'you hear?"

At last the Chancellor found words, and beset his son with a torrent of blasphemy, and with foul-mouthed abuse.

"Be quiet!" said the other, standing up to him. "How dare you speak to me like that! It's no good trying to bully me now."

"By God, I'll knock you down."

Rallington thrust his face close to his father's, and for a moment fear seized the old man. Here at length was some one whom he could not cow, and he hated his son.

"You'd better not touch me. You can't thrash me now as you could when I was a boy. I recommend you to take great care."

Lord Spratte raised his hands, but a trembling came suddenly upon him, so that he could not move.

"Get out of my house," he screamed. "Get out of my house."

"I'm only too glad to go."

The arteries beat in the old man's head so that he thought some horrible thing would happen to him. He poured out brandy and drank it, but it tasted like water. He sat for hours with clenched fists and scowling brow; and at last with a savage laugh he took his will and with his own hand wrote a codicil in which he deprived his eldest son of every penny he could. This relieved him and he breathed more freely. Presently he called his family together and told them without a word of explanation that Rallington was his son no longer.

"If any of you mention his name, or if I hear that you have had any communication with him, you shall go as he went."

The pair never met again, for Rallington went abroad and died, unmarried, one month before his father. Thomas, the next son, who had been known all his life as Tommy Tiddler, succeeded the Chancellor as second Earl Spratte of Beachcombe.

But the excellent Theodore, with proper devotion, took care in his biography not even to hint at this characteristic violence. He wrote with a flowing, somewhat pompous style; and the moral pointed by these two handsome volumes was that with uprightness, sobriety, and due allegiance to the Church by law established, it was possible to reach the highest honours. The learned Canon traced the ancestry of his family to very remote periods. He had no difficulty in convincing himself that the plebeian surname was but a vulgar error for des Prats; and to the outspoken ridicule of his elder brother, was able after much study to announce that a member of the English branch of the Montmorencys had assumed the name in the seventeenth century upon his marriage with a French heiress. With these distinguished antecedents it was no wonder that Josiah Spratte should appear a benevolent old gentleman of mild temper and pious disposition, apt to express himself in well-balanced periods. He would have made an excellent churchwarden or a secretary to charitable institutions, but why precisely he should have become Lord Chancellor of England nowhere appeared. In short, the eloquent divine, with the best intentions in the world, wrote a life of his father which was not only perfectly untrue, but also exceedingly tedious.

The book had a certain success with old ladies, who put it beside their works of devotion and had it read to them in hours of mental distress. Sometimes, when they were persons of uncommon importance, the Canon himself consented to read to them; and then, so spirited was his delivery, so well-modulated his voice, it seemed as improving as one of his own sermons. But the Life and Letters certainly had no more assiduous nor enthusiastic reader than the author thereof.

"I don't think I'm a vain man," he remarked, "but I can't help feeling this is exactly how a biography ought to be written."

There was a knock at the door, and the Canon, replacing the volume at which he had glanced, took out in its stead the first book of Hooker's Ecclesiastical Polity. He had far too keen a sense of decorum to appear one man to the world and to his immediate relatives another. No unforeseen accident had ever found him other than self-contained, oratorical, and didactic. Not even his family was privileged to see him en robe de chambre.

It was his son who knocked. Lionel had been taking an early service at St. Gregory's, and had not yet seen his father.

"Come in, come in," said the Canon. "Good morning, Lionel."

"I hope I'm not disturbing you, father. I want to book some certificates."

"You can never disturb me when you are fulfilling the duties of your office, my boy. Pray sit down."

He put the Ecclesiastical Polity open on the desk.

"Hulloa, are you reading this?" asked the curate. "I've not looked at it since I was at Oxford."

"Then you make a mistake, Lionel. Hooker's Ecclesiastical Polity is not only a monument of the English Church, but also a masterwork of the English language. That is my complaint with the clergy of the present day, that they neglect the great productions of their fathers. Stevenson you read, and you read Renan, atheist though he is; but Hooker you have not looked at since you were at Oxford."

"I see that Andover is dead, father," said Lionel, to change the conversation.

"I look upon it as an uncommon happy release."

"I wonder if they really will offer you the bishopric?"

"My dear boy, that is not a subject upon which I allow my thoughts to dwell. I will not conceal from you that, as the youngest surviving son of the late Lord Chancellor, I think I have some claims upon my country. And I have duties towards it as well, so that if the bishopric is offered to me I shall not hesitate to accept. You remember St. Paul's words to Timothy? This is a true saying, if a man desire the office of a bishop he desireth a good work. But in these matters there is so much ignoble wire-pulling, so much backstairs influence to which my character is not suited and to which I could not bring myself to descend."

Presently, however, when Canon Spratte strolled along Piccadilly on the way to his club, it occurred to him that the day before he had given his tailor an order for two pairs of trousers. His circumstances had taught him neither to spend money recklessly, nor to despise a certain well-bred economy; and it was by no means impossible that he would have no use for those particular articles of clothing. He walked up Savile Row.

"Mr. Marsden, will you inquire whether those garments I ordered yesterday have been cut yet?"

The tailor passed the question down his speaking-tube.

"No, sir," he said. "Not yet."

"Then will you delay them till further notice?"

"Certainly, sir."

Canon Spratte was going out of the shop when he noticed on a fashion plate the costume of a bishop.

"Ah, do you make gaiters, Mr. Marsden?" said he, stopping.

"Yes, sir."

"They're very difficult things to cut. So many of my friends wear very ill-fitting gaiters. Fine day, isn't it? Good-morning."

III

WHEN Canon Spratte reached the Athenæum he found a note waiting for him.

My Dear Canon,

I should very much like to have a little talk with you. I find it difficult to say in so many words upon what topic, but perhaps you will guess. I think it better to see you before I do anything further, and therefore should be grateful if you could give me five minutes as soon as possible.

Yours ever faithfully,
Wroxham.

He read it, and a smile of self-satisfaction played quickly on his lips. He divined at once that the writer wished to ask Winnie to marry him.

"I foresaw it when the boy was fourteen," he exclaimed.

His own wife had died ten years before. She was a pale, mild creature, and had been somewhat overwhelmed by her husband's greatness. When he was still a curate, handsome and debonair, the Canon had fallen in love with the youngest daughter of Lord Frampstone. It was an alliance, (Theodore Spratte would never have condescended to a marriage,) of which the Chancellor thoroughly approved; and the girl, dazzled by her suitor's courtly brilliance, had succumbed at once to his fascinations. She remained dazzled to the end of her life. He never unbent. He treated her always as though she were a congregation. Even in the privacies of domestic life he was talking to a multitude; and his wife, if sometimes she wished he would descend to her level and vouchsafe to be familiar, never ceased blindly to admire him. She sighed for a little simple love, but the Canon could not forget that he was a son of a great Lord Chancellor and she the daughter of a noble house. She was confused by his oratorical outbursts, his wit, his grandiose ways; and gradually, unnoticed in the white brilliance of her husband's glory, she vanished out of existence. The Canon's only complaint was that his wife had never lived up to the position which was hers by right. She cared nothing for social success, and was happiest in the bosom of her family.

“Upon my word, my dear, you might as well be the wife of a dissenting minister,” he exclaimed often.

But her death gave him an opportunity to prove his own regard and to make up for her previous shortcomings. He ordered a funeral of the utmost magnificence; and the gentle lady, who had longed only for peace, was buried with as great parade as if she had been a princess of the blood. On a large brass tablet, emblazoned with his own arms and with those of her family, the lamenting husband, who prided himself not a little on his skilful Latinity, placed a Ciceronian epitaph which caused amazement and admiration in all beholders.

The recollection of his wife flashed at this moment through the Canon’s mind, and putting his own sentiments into her meek breast, he flourished the letter and chuckled to himself.

“I wish she were alive to see this day.”

Lord Wroxham, left fatherless in early boyhood, was head of a family than which there was none in England more ancient and more distinguished. Canon Spratte called a servant.

“Will you ask the porter if Lord Wroxham is in the club?”

“Yes, sir. I saw him come in half-an-hour ago.”

“Ha!”

Canon Spratte put a cigarette between his lips and jauntily went to the smoking-room. He caught sight at once of his prospective son-in-law, but made no sign that he observed him. He strolled across the room.

“Canon Spratte!” said the young man, rising and turning very red.

“Ah, my dear boy,” said the Canon, cordially holding out his hand. “Are you here? I’m delighted to see you. I was just going to write you a note.”

Wroxham was a young man of five-and-twenty, slender and of moderate height, with short crisp hair and a small moustache. His eyes were prominent and short-sighted, and he wore gold-rimmed pince-nez. His appearance was a little insignificant, but his pleasant, earnest face, if not handsome, was very kindly. He was nervous, and had evidently no great facility in expressing himself.

Canon Spratte, aware of his confusion, took his arm and led him to a more secluded place.

“Come and sit in the window, dear boy, and tell me what it is you wish to say.”

When the Canon desired to be charming, none could excel him. There was such a sympathetic warmth in his manner that, if you were not irritated by a slightly patronizing air, your heart never failed to go out to him.

"Have a cigarette," he said, producing a golden case of considerable value. "Give me a match, there's a good fellow."

He beamed on the youth, but still Wroxham hesitated.

"You got my note, Canon?"

"Yes, yes. So charming of you to write to me. I've known you so long, dear boy—if there's anything I can do for you, command me."

Wroxham had often come with Lionel from Eton to spend part of his holidays in the Canon's hospitable house.

"Well, the fact is—I want to ask Winnie to marry me, with your permission."

Canon Spratte restrained the smile of triumph which struggled to gain possession of his mouth. When he answered, his manner was perfectly sympathetic, but somewhat grave as befitted the occasion.

"My dear Harry, I will not conceal from you that your sentiments have not been altogether hidden from me. And you will understand that if I had not approved of them I should scarcely have allowed you to come so frequently to my house."

Wroxham smiled, but found nothing very apposite to say.

"I have had for years the very greatest affection for you; and of late, since you took your seat in the House of Lords, I have had also esteem and admiration. It is an excellent sign when a young man of your position throws himself so earnestly into affairs of State. I think you have a great future before you."

He put up his hand to request silence, as he saw the other wished to make some remark. Canon Spratte did not suffer interruption kindly.

"But in these matters one is a father first and last. I have reason to believe that you are a steady young man, without vices, and I think you have an excellent temper, than which nothing is more necessary in married life. But you must allow me to inquire a little into your circumstances."

The young man very simply explained that he possessed three houses, a great many acres of land, and an income of twenty thousand a year. Canon Spratte listened gravely.

"I should like to leave all the affairs about settlements in your hands, Canon. I'll do whatever you think fit."

"All that sounds very satisfactory," answered the Canon, at last. "I am not the man to go into pecuniary details. Thank God, I can honestly say I'm not mercenary, and I think we can leave all business details to our respective lawyers. My dear boy, I give you full permission to pay your addresses to Winnie."

Wroxham flushed, and taking off his glasses, rubbed them with a handkerchief.

"Do you think she cares for me?"

The Canon took both his hands.

"My dear fellow, you need have no fear on that point. Of course, I leave my children complete liberty of action, but I don't think I am indiscreet in assuring you that Winnie is—well, very fond of you."

"I'm so glad," said Wroxham, a happy smile breaking on his lips.

"Come to luncheon to-morrow and have a talk with my little girl afterwards. I'll arrange it so that you shall be undisturbed."

"It's awfully good of you."

"Not at all! Not at all! But now I really must be running off. I'm lunching with Lady Vizard, to meet the Princess of Wartburg-Hochstein."

IV

WINNIE went to Mr. Railing's temperance meeting by herself. When she was setting out to go home, with somewhat marked deliberation, the Socialist joined her.

"Your father has asked me to come to tea."

"I know," she answered. "Shall we walk back together?"

Bertram Railing was three-and-twenty, and Winnie had not exaggerated too grossly when she vowed he was as beautiful as a Greek god. He was very dark, but his skin, smoother than polished ivory, had the glowing colour of Titian's young Adonis; and his hair, worn long and admirably curling, his fine sincere eyes, were dark too. With his broad forehead, his straight nose, his well-shaped, sensual mouth, he was indeed very handsome; and there was a squareness about his jaw which suggested besides much strength of character. His expression was sombre; but when, fired with enthusiasm, he spoke of any subject that deeply interested him, his face grew very mobile. He wore a blue serge suit, a red tie, and a low collar which showed his powerful, statuesque neck. If he could not be altogether unconscious of his good looks, he was certainly indifferent to them. His whole life was given up to a passionate striving for reform, and his absorbing interest in the improvement of the people allowed no room for trifling, unworthy thoughts. The strenuous pursuit of the ideal gave him a fascination far greater than that of his wonderful face.

"Did you like my lecture?" he asked, as they walked side by side.

Winnie looked at him, her eyes filled suddenly with tears.

"Yes."

It was all she could say, but Railing smiled with pleasure. In this one word was so much feeling that it pleased him more than all the applause he had received.

"You can't imagine what I felt while I was listening to you," she said at last.

"If I spoke well it was because I knew your eyes were upon me."

"I felt perfectly hysterical. I had to bite my lips to prevent myself from crying."

They walked in silence, each occupied with tumultuous thoughts. His presence was enchanting to Winnie, and yet the joy of it was almost painful. A marvellous change had come upon her during the last few days, and life was altogether new. The world seemed strangely full of emotion, and the parts of the earth, in the spring sunshine, sang to one another joyful songs.

"You've done so much for me," she murmured, happy to confess her inmost thoughts. "Until I knew you I was so selfish and stupid. But now everything is different. I want to help you in your work. I want to work too."

For a moment, finding nothing to say, he gazed at her. His brown eyes, so strong and full of meaning, looked into hers gravely; and hers were blue and tender. But the silence grew unendurable, and flushing, the girl looked down.

"Why don't you speak?"

"I think I'm afraid," he answered, and there was a tremor in his voice.

She felt that his heart was beating as quickly as her own.

"Who am I that you should be afraid?" she whispered.

He gave a sigh that was half joy, half sorrow; and clenched his hands in the effort to master himself. But the girl's sweet freshness rose to his nostrils like the scent of the earth in the morning after the rain, and his poor wits were all aflame.

"If I've done anything for you," he said at last, "you've done a thousand times more for me. When first I met you I was utterly discouraged. The way seemed so hard. It was so difficult to make any progress. And then you filled me with hope."

He began to speak hurriedly, and Winnie listened to his words as though they were some new evangel. He told her of his plans and of his enthusiastic ambition to get the people the power that was theirs by right. When he spoke of wages and of labour, of Co-operative Associations and of Trades Unions, it sounded like music in her ears. He told her of Lassalle's fevered life, of Marx' ceaseless struggle, of the pitying anguish of Carl Marlo. He spoke so earnestly, with such a vehemence of phrase, that Winnie, used to the sonorous platitudes of her father, was carried out as it were into the bottomless sea of life. After the artificiality wherein she had lived, these new doctrines, so boldly regardless of consequence, eager only for justice, were like the fresh air of heaven: her pulse beat more rapidly, and she knew that beyond her narrow sphere was a freer world. Railing spoke of the people; and the human beings whom she had classed disdainfully as the lower orders, gained flesh and blood in her imagination. He spoke of their passions and their misery, of their strength, their vice and squalor. The many-headed crowd grew picturesque and coloured. Winnie was seized on a sudden with the desire to go into their midst; and gaining a new strength of purpose, she felt already a greater self-reliance. Then more slowly, as though her presence were almost forgotten, but with the same intense conviction, the young Socialist spoke of the Nazarene who was the friend of the poor, the outcast, and the leper. Winnie had known Him only as the mainstay of an opulent and established Church. In her mind He was strangely connected with pews of pitch-pine, a fashionable congregation in Sabbath garments, and the imposing presence of her father. She learned now, as though it were a new thing, that the Christ was a ragged labourer, one with the carpenter who worked at St. Gregory's Vicarage, the mason carrying a hod, and the scavenger who swept the streets. In these simple words she found a reality that had never appeared in her father's rhetoric.

"And that's why I call myself a Christian Socialist," he said, "because I believe that to these two belong the future—to Christ and to the people."

Winnie did not answer, and they walked again in silence.

"Do you despise me?" she cried at length. "Do you think I'm vain and foolish? I'm so ashamed of myself."

He looked at her with those passionate eyes of his, and his whole heart yearned for her.

"You know what I think of you," he said.

They were approaching the Vicarage and time was very short. Winnie threw off all reserve.

"I want to help you, I want to work with you, I hate the life I lead at home. I'm not a woman, I'm only a foolish doll. Take me away from it."

The blood rushed to his face and the flame of an ecstatic happiness lit up his eyes. He could scarcely believe that he had heard aright.

"Do you mean that?" he cried, hastily. "Oh, don't play with me. Don't you know that I love you? I love you with all the strength I've got. When I'm away from you it's madness; I can think of nothing but you all day, all night."

Winnie sighed.

"I'm so glad to hear you say that."

"Do you care for me at all?" he insisted, doubting still.

"Yes, I love you with my whole soul."

When they reached St. Gregory's Vicarage, the Canon greeted Railing with effusion.

"My dear Mr. Railing, it's so kind of you to come. Permit me to introduce you to my sister. Mr. Railing is the author of that admirable and much-discussed book, The Future of Socialism."

"And what is the future of Socialism?" asked Lady Sophia, politely.

"It took me three hundred pages to answer that question," he replied, with a smile.

"Then you must allow me to give you some tea at once."

Winnie went up to her uncle, who had been lunching quietly with his sister, but he put out a deprecating hand.

"You'd better not kiss me after being at a temperance meeting," he said. "I'm awfully afraid of catchin' things. I always think it's such a mercy there are no poor people at St. Gregory's."

"D'you think they're all infectious?" smiled Railing.

"One can never tell, you know. I always recommend Theodore to sprinkle himself with Keating's Powder when he's been marrying the lower classes."

Railing tightened his lips at the flippant remark, and Winnie, watching him, was ashamed of the frivolous atmosphere into which she had brought him. It seemed to her suddenly that these people among whom till now she had lived contentedly, were but play-actors repeating carelessly the words they had learnt by rote. That drawing-room, with its smart chintzes and fashionable Sheraton, was a stuffy prison in which she could not breathe. She knew a hundred parlours which differed from this one hardly at all: the same flowers were on the same tables, arranged in the same way, the same books lay here and there, the same periodicals. In one and all the same life was led; and it was artificial, conventional, untrue. She and her friends were performing an elaborate but trivial play, some of the scenes whereof took place in a dining-room, some in a ball-room, others in the park, and some in fashionable shops. But round this vast theatre was a great stone wall, and outside it men and women and children swarmed in vast numbers, and lived and loved and starved and worked and died.

Bertram turned to Canon Spratte.

"I see that one of our most ardent champions in the cause of temperance has just died," he said.

"Bishop Andover?" exclaimed the Canon. "Very sad, very sad! I knew him well. Sophia is of opinion that he was the most learned of our bishops."

"He'll be a great loss."

"Oh, a great loss!" cried the Canon, with conviction. "I was terribly distressed when I heard of the sad event."

"Are there any golf-links at Barchester?" asked Lord Spratte, with a glance at his brother.

Railing looked at him with surprise, naturally not catching the purport of this question.

"I really don't know." Then he gave Canon Spratte a smile. "I hear it's being suggested that you may go there."

Canon Spratte received the suggestion without embarrassment.

"It would require a great deal to tear me away from St. Gregory's," he answered, gravely. "I'm thoroughly attached to the parish."

"I don't know what they would do without you here."

"Of course no man is indispensable in this world; but I don't know that I should consider myself fit to take so large and important a See as that of Barchester."

Winnie took her uncle some tea and sat down beside him.

"What d'you think of Mr. Railing?" she asked, abruptly.

"Smells of public spirit, don't he? He's the sort of chap that has statistics scribbled all over his shirt-cuffs." His jaw dropped. "And his shirt-cuffs take off."

"Why shouldn't they?" asked Winnie, flushing.

"My dear, there's no reason at all. Nor have I ever been able to discover why you shouldn't eat peas with a knife or assassinate your grandmother. But I notice there is a prejudice against these things."

"I think he's the most wonderful man I've ever seen in my life."

"Do you, by Jove!" cried Lord Spratte. "Have you told your father?"

Winnie gave him a defiant look.

"No, but I mean to. You all think I'm still a child. You none of you understand that I'm a woman."

"I notice your sex generally claims to be misunderstood when it has a mind to do something particularly foolish."

"I wish you had heard him speak. I could hardly control myself."

"Because he dropped his aitches?"

"Of course not. Can't you see he's a gentleman?"

"I'm so short-sighted," replied Lord Spratte, dryly. "And I haven't my opera-glasses with me."

Winnie rose impatiently and walked over to her father.

Lord Spratte watched her with some curiosity, and he caught Railing's glance as she came up. His lips formed themselves into a whistle. He chuckled as he thought of Theodore's consternation if what he suspected proved true.

"I'm so sorry that a perfectly unavoidable engagement prevented me from coming to hear you speak," the Canon said, in his politest way.

"It was splendid," cried Winnie, enthusiastically, forgetting already her uncle's sneer. "I'm never going to touch alcohol again."

Railing looked at her gratefully, and his eyes were full of passionate admiration.

"Capital, capital!" burst out the Canon, patting his friend on the back. "You're an orator, Railing."

"You should have seen the audience," said Winnie. "While Mr. Railing spoke you could have heard a pin drop. And when he finished they broke into such a storm of applause that I thought the roof was coming down."

"They were all very kind and very appreciative," said Railing, modestly.

Lady Sophia, raising her eyebrows, looked with astonishment at her niece, than whom generally no one could be more composed. Winnie was very apt to think enthusiasm a mark of ill-breeding, and the display of genuine feeling proof of the worst possible taste. But now she was too happy to care what her aunt thought, and seeing the look, answered it boldly.

"You should have seen the people, Aunt Sophia. They crowded round him and wouldn't let him go. Every one wanted to shake hands with him."

"It's wonderful how people are carried away by real eloquence," said the Canon, in his impressive fashion. "You must really come and hear me preach, Mr. Railing. Of course I don't pretend to have any gifts comparable to yours, but I'm preparing a course of sermons on Christian Socialism which may conceivably interest you."

"I should like to hear you," answered the other, putting as usual his whole soul into the casual conversation. To Lady Sophia his strenuous way rang out of tune with the rest of the company, but Winnie thought him the only real man she had ever known. "The clergy ought to be in the forefront of every movement."

"Yes," said the Canon, with that glance at the ancestral portrait which so often preluded a flourish of oratory. "Advance and progress have ever been my watchwords. I think I can truthfully say that my family has always been in the vanguard of any movement for the advantage of the working-classes."

"From the days of the Montmorencys down to our father, the late Lord Chancellor of England," put in Lord Spratte, gravely.

Theodore gave the head of his house a look of some vexation, but drew himself to his full height.

"As my brother amiably reminds me, my ancestor, Aubrey de

Montmorency, was killed while fighting for the freedom of the people, in the year 1642. And his second son, from whom we are directly descended...." Lady Sophia gave a significant cough, but the Canon went on firmly, "was beheaded by James II for resisting the tyranny of that Popish and despotic sovereign."

None could deny that the sentence was rhythmical. The delivery was perfect.

Presently Railing got up.

"What, must you go already?" cried the Canon. "Well, well, I daresay you're busy. You must come and see us again, soon; I want to have a long talk with you. And don't forget to come and hear me preach."

When Railing took Winnie's hand, she felt it almost impossible to command herself.

"I shall see you again to-morrow?" she whispered.

"I shan't think of anything else till then," he said.

His dark eyes, so passionately tender, burnt like fire in her heart. Railing went out.

"Intelligent fellow!" said Canon Spratte, as the door closed behind him. "I like him very much. Remarkably brilliant, isn't he, Sophia?"

"My dear Theodore, how could I judge?" she answered, somewhat irritably. "You never let him get a word in. He seemed an intelligent listener."

"My dear Sophia, I may have faults," laughed the Canon. "We all have faults—even you, my dear. But no one has ever accused me of usurping more than my fair share of the conversation. I daresay he was a little shy."

"I daresay!" said Lady Sophia, dryly.

V

THE same evening, before going to his room to dress for dinner at the Hollingtons, Canon Spratte wrote to an acquaintance who was clerical correspondent for an important paper.

My Dear Mr. Wilson,

I wish you would announce in your admirable Journal that there is no truth whatever in the rumour that I have been offered the vacant bishopric of Barchester. This, however, gives me an opportunity to say how thoroughly I condemn the modern practice of assigning this and that post, in the wildest, most improbable fashion, to all sorts and conditions of men. In these days of self-advertisement, I suppose it is too much to ask that people should keep silent on the positions to which they expect themselves or their friends to be elevated, but I cannot help thinking such a proceeding would be at once more decorous and more discreet.

Yours most faithfully,
Theodore Spratte.

While changing, he remembered that flippant, disparaging remark which Lady Sophia had made the day before about his calves. He looked at himself in the glass and smiled with good-humoured scorn.

"They think I couldn't wear gaiters," he murmured. "I fancy there are few bishops who've got better legs than I have."

They were indeed well-shaped and muscular, for Canon Spratte, wisely, took abundant exercise.

"I think it's rather chilly to-night, Ponsonby," he said. "Will you bring me my fur coat."

He put it on, and holding himself with a sort of dashing serenity, looked again in the glass. It would have been absurd not to recognize that he was a person of handsome and attractive presence. Few men can wear very elaborate garments without being ridiculous, but Canon Spratte was made for pompous, magnificent habiliments.

"A man in a fur coat is a noble animal," he said, with deep conviction. "Is the carriage there?"

Canon Spratte was at his best in feminine society. He used women with a charming urbanity which reminded you of a past age when good manners were still cultivated by the great ones of the earth. There was a polite suppleness about his backbone, a caressing intonation of his voice, which captivated the least susceptible. He was an ornament to any party, for he never failed to say a clever thing at the necessary moment. He could flatter the young by his courtliness and amuse the old by his repartee. The triumphant air with which he entered the Hollingtons' drawing-room sufficed to impress you with his powers. It was certainly an odd contrast between the flamboyant style of the Canon of Tercanbury and the clumsy shuffling of Lord Stonehenge, ill-dressed and untidy, who immediately followed.

To his great good fortune Canon Spratte found he was to take down to dinner Lady Patricia, the Prime Minister's daughter. He could be brilliant and talkative, but on occasion he could be also a witty listener; and this useful art he employed now to the best advantage. None knew what self-restraint it needed for Canon Spratte to seem a little dull, but he was aware that Lady Patricia shared her father's predilection for undangerous mediocrity. He heard what she said with grave interest. He asked intelligent questions. He went so far as to demand her advice on a matter wherein he had no intention of following any opinion but his own. Lady Patricia gained the impression that there was no one in the world at that moment whom he wanted to see more than herself, and she talked with a fluency that was as unusual as it was pleasing. She was a woman who found topics of conversation with difficulty, and so felt uncommonly pleased with herself. She could not help thinking the Canon a man of considerable ability. And the contrast between him and her other neighbour was altogether to Canon Spratte's advantage. Lady Hollington had the fashionable craze for asking literary and artistic persons to her parties. They take the place in a democratic age of the buffoons whom princes formerly kept in their houses, and are a luxury which the most economical can afford. But the novelist who now claimed Lady Patricia's attention, entertained her with his theories upon art and literature; and since she knew nothing of either, and cared less, the poor lady was immoderately bored.

The Canon was delighted to find on his left an old friend of his. Mrs. Fitzherbert was a handsome widow of five-and-forty, with singularly fine teeth, and these a charming smile gave her an opportunity of displaying with some frequency. None knew whether

her keen sense of humour was due to the excellence of her teeth, or whether her teeth were so noticeable on account of this acute perception of the ridiculous.

"I'm doubly favoured by the gods this evening," said Canon Spratte. "If I were a Papist I would offer a candle of gratitude to my patron saint. I didn't know I should be so fortunate as to meet you nor so lucky as to sit by your side."

"It's taken you some time to avail yourself of the privilege of speaking to me," she answered, glancing at the menu.

"I wanted to appease the pangs of my hunger first, so that I could devote myself to the pleasure of your conversation with an undistracted mind."

"Then you agree with me, that a man is only quite human when he's eaten his dinner?" she smiled.

"My thoughts are never so ethereal as when my body is occupied with the process of digestion," the Canon replied, ironically.

He thought that Mrs. Fitzherbert wore uncommonly well. She had always been a fine creature, but he had never guessed that the girl of somewhat overwhelming physique whom he had known a quarter of a century before, would turn into this stately woman. The years only increased her attractiveness, and she had reason to look upon the common foes of mankind as her particular friends. She held herself with the assurance of a woman who has enjoyed masculine admiration. The Canon's eyes rested with approval on the gown which displayed to advantage her beautiful figure.

These flattering reflections were, perhaps, obvious on his face, for the lady smiled.

"You may make it," she said, with a flash of her exquisite teeth.

"What?" asked the Canon, innocently opening his eyes.

"The compliment that's on the tip of your tongue."

"I think you grow handsomer every day," he answered, without hesitation.

"Thank you. And now tell me about Sophia and the children."

"I'd much sooner talk about you," said the Canon, gallantly.

"My dear friend, we've known one another too long. For flattery to be pleasing one must be convinced, at least for a moment, that it's sincere, and you know I've never concealed from you my belief that you're the most desperate humbug I've ever known."

"You put me at my ease at once," he retorted, smiling and not in the least disconcerted. "But I'm sorry you're so vain."

"Do you think I'm that?"

"Certainly. It's only because your inner consciousness tells you such agreeable things that you won't listen to my timid observations."

Mrs. Fitzherbert looked at him quickly and wondered if his memory was as bad as he pretended. She did not feel it necessary to recall exactly how many years it was since first they met, but she was a girl then, and Theodore the handsomest man she had ever seen. Her maiden fancy was speedily captured, and for a season they danced together, philandered, and sauntered in the park. Unwisely, she took him with all seriousness. She remembered still a certain afternoon in July when they met in Kensington Gardens; the sunshine and the careful trees, the dainty flowers, gave the scene all the graceful elegance of a picture by the adorable Watteau. She was going into the country next day, and her young heart beat in the most romantic fashion because she thought Theodore would seize the opportunity to declare his passion. But instead, he asked if she could keep a secret, and told her he had just become engaged to Dorothy Frampstone. She had not forgotten the smile with which she congratulated him and the lightness wherewith she hid the terrible anguish that consumed her. For six weeks she saw the world through a mist of tears, but pride forbade her to refuse Dorothy's invitation to be bridesmaid at the wedding, and here she met Captain Fitzherbert. He fell in love with her at first sight and she married him out of pique, only to discover that he was a perfectly charming fellow. She soon grew devoted to him and never ceased to thank Heaven for her escape from Theodore. The only emotion that touched her then was curiosity. She would have given much to learn the reason of his behaviour. But she never knew whether the handsome curate had really cared, and thrown her over only because a more eligible bride presented herself; or whether, blinded by her own devotion, she had mistaken for love attentions which were due merely to a vivacious temperament. She did not meet Theodore Spratte again till she had been for some time a widow. Captain Fitzherbert was stationed in various parts of the world, and his wife came rarely to England. Then he fell ill, and for several years she nursed him on the Riviera and in Italy. But when at last his death released her, Mrs. Fitzherbert sought to regain her calmness of mind after the long exhaustion of his illness, by distant journeys to those places where she had spent her happy married life. It was not till she took a house in London, three years before this, that she ran against Canon Spratte casually at a dinner-party.

She was pleased to see him, but noted with amusement that the sight did not agitate her in the smallest degree. She could scarcely believe that once his appearance in a room sufficed to make her pulse beat at double its normal rate, while the touch of his hand sent the blood rushing to her cheeks.

Mrs. Fitzherbert had acquired a certain taste for original sensations, and it diverted her to meet again in this fashion the lover of her youth. She wanted to know how he had fared and what sort of man he was become. Outwardly he had altered but little; he was as tall and as handsome, and had still the curly hair which she had so desperately adored. The years had dealt amiably with him, and she was delighted that on her side the change was all for the better. She could not deny now that at eighteen she must have been a lumbersome, awkward girl; and a young man could not guess that time and a discreet skill in the artifices of the toilet would transform her into a striking woman whom men turned round in the street to admire. At the end of their first conversation Canon Spratte asked if he might call upon her, and two days later had tea at the new house in Norfolk Street. From these beginnings a somewhat intimate acquaintance had arisen, and now Mrs. Fitzherbert was on the best of terms with all his family. The winter before she had asked Winnie to come to the Riviera with her, and the affectionate father had agreed that no better companion for his daughter could possibly be chosen. He disclosed to her now the great news of Wroxham's proposal.

"You must be very proud and pleased," said Mrs. Fitzherbert.

"Of course it's always satisfactory for a father to see his daughter happily married. He's an excellent fellow and quite comfortably off."

"So I've always understood," she answered with a smile, amused because the Canon would not acknowledge that Wroxham was far and away the best parti of the season.

Mrs. Fitzherbert had quickly taken Theodore's measure, and it was a curious satisfaction, sweet and bitter at the same time, to find defects of character in the man who had once appeared so romantic a hero. She looked upon him with oddly mingled feelings. Her sense of humour caused her vastly to enjoy the rich comedy of his behaviour, but she preserved for him, almost against her will, a certain tenderness. He had made her suffer so much. She saw that he was often absurd, but liked him none the less. Though she discovered the feet of clay, she could not forget that once he had seemed a golden idol. She was willing to forgive the faults she now saw clearly, rather than think she had loved quite foolishly. The Canon felt her sympathy and opened his heart as to an old friend with a frankness he showed to no one else. The smile in her handsome eyes never warned him that she tore him to shreds, not unkindly but with deliberation, piece by piece.

Mrs. Fitzherbert asked how long Winnie had been engaged, and was somewhat astounded at his answer.

"He hasn't spoken to her yet, but we've talked it over between us, he and I, and he's to come to luncheon to-morrow to make his declaration."

"Then Winnie hasn't been consulted?" she exclaimed.

"My dear lady, do you imagine for a moment she'll refuse?"

Mrs. Fitzherbert laughed.

"No, I frankly don't. She's not her father's child for nothing."

"I look upon it as completely settled, and then I shall have only Lionel to dispose of. Of course I'm far more anxious about him. In all probability he will succeed to the title, and it's important that he should marry a suitable person."

"What do you mean by that?"

He looked at her and smiled.

"Well, you know, the Sprattes are poor, and if Lionel has no children the peerage will be extinct. I can allow him to marry no one who hasn't considerable means and every appearance of promising a healthy family."

"Would it surprise you very much to know that the matter is already somewhat out of your hands? Unless I'm very much mistaken, Lionel is making up his mind to propose to Gwendolen Durant; and unless I'm equally mistaken, Gwendolen Durant is making up her mind to accept him."

"You amaze me," cried the Canon. "I've never even heard of this person."

"Oh, yes, you have; she's the only daughter of Sir John Durant, the brewer."

"Monstrous! I will never allow Lionel to marry any one of the sort."

"I believe he's rather in love with her."

"Good heavens, it's just as easy for him to fall in love with a girl of good family. I did, and upon my word I can't see why he shouldn't follow his father's example."

"The Durants are very nice people, and—prolific," smiled Mrs. Fitzherbert. "Gwendolen had six brothers, three of whom are still alive, and her father was one of ten children."

"Sir John is only a Jubilee baronet. I would as soon he were a city knight."

"On the other hand, he proposes to give his daughter one hundred and fifty thousand pounds as her marriage portion."

Theodore Spratte turned right round and stared at Mrs. Fitzherbert.

"That's a very large sum," he smiled.

"It certainly may help the course of true love to run smoothly."

"No wonder that Lionel was disinclined to accept the Bishop's advice to become a total abstainer," the Canon chuckled. "It would really be rather uncivil if he has matrimonial designs on a brewer's daughter."

He thoughtfully sipped his wine and allowed this information to settle. Mrs. Fitzherbert turned to somebody else, and the Canon was left for a couple of moments to his own reflections. Presently she smiled at him again.

"Well?"

"I'll tell you what I wish you would do. I understand you are deputed to find out my views upon the subject."

"Nothing of the sort," she interrupted. "Sir John cares nothing for your views. He is a merchant of the old school, and looks upon himself as every man's equal. I don't know whether he has thought for a moment of Gwendolen's future, but you may be quite sure he won't consider it a very signal honour that she should marry Lionel."

"You express yourself with singular bluntness," answered the Canon, mildly.

"Nor do I know that the young things have settled anything. I merely tell you what my eyes have suggested to me. If you like, I'll ask the Durants to luncheon, and you can see them for yourself."

"But tell me, does she lead one to imagine that she'll——" he hesitated for a moment, but made a dash for it, "breed well?"

"My dear Canon, I never considered her from that point of view," laughed Mrs. Fitzherbert.

Canon Spratte smiled and shrugged his shoulders.

"One must be practical. Of course a great change has come over the opinion of society with regard to the position of merchants, and one mustn't lag behind the times."

"A Conservative member of Parliament is still an object of admiration to many," murmured Mrs. Fitzherbert.

"Well, well, I'm not the man to stand in the way of my children's happiness, and if I find that Lionel loves the girl, I promise you to put no obstacle in his way."

Lady Hollington rose from her chair, and with a rustling sweep of silk skirts, with a quick gleam of diamonds, the ladies followed one another from the dining-room. Their host took his glass and moved round the table to sit by his most distinguished guest. But Canon Spratte, like a wise man, had already seized the opportunity. He drew his chair near that of Lord Stonehenge. The Prime Minister, obese and somnolent, turned upon him for a moment his dull, suspicious eyes, and then sunk his head strangely into his vast corpulence.

"I'm sorry to see that poor Andover is dead," said the Canon, blandly.

His neighbour, meditative as a cow chewing the cud, made no sign that he heard the observation; but Canon Spratte was by no means disconcerted.

"He'll be a great loss and most difficult to replace," he continued. "They say he was the most learned of our bishops. I was excessively distressed when I heard of the sad event."

"What did he die of?" asked the Prime Minister, indifferently.

"Oh, he was a very old man," promptly replied the other, who had no idea to what fell disease the late Bishop of Barchester had succumbed. "My own conviction is that bishops ought to retire like ambassadors. A bishop should be a man of restless strength, active and versatile; he should be ready to put his hand to anything. To be a bishop you want as much energy and resource as if you were manager of the Army and Navy Stores."

"Who is the manager of the Army and Navy Stores?" asked Lord Stonehenge.

Theodore Spratte smiled politely, but thought none the less that the Prime Minister was growing very stupid.

"Thank heaven, I shall never be as fat as that," he said to himself, and added aloud: "I believe Andover was appointed by Mr. Gladstone."

"How very large these grapes are!" said Lord Stonehenge, looking heavily at the dish of fruit in front of him.

"Yes," said the Canon undisturbed, "my father, the Chancellor, used to grow very fine grapes at Beachcombe. You know, of course, that he held very decided views about the political opinions of the bishops."

A slight movement went through the Prime Minister's colossal frame, like a peristaltic wave passing along the coiled length of a boa-constrictor. Canon Spratte seemed to him like an agile fly that settled on every exposed place, and alit elsewhere as soon as it was brushed away. Just as all roads lead to Rome, every comment that Lord Stonehenge made appeared to bear directly upon the vacant See.

"And I cannot help thoroughly agreeing with him," proceeded the Canon. "My view is that the bishops should be imbued with Conservative principles. The episcopal bench, I always think, should be a stronghold of Tory tradition, and if you come to think of it, the very nature of things accords with my conviction."

Lord Stonehenge gave no sign of disagreement, which was sufficient excuse for Canon Spratte to state at length his laudable opinions. Presently, however, Lord Hollington proposed that they should go upstairs, and on their way the Canon shot his last bolt.

"By the bye, I was just talking to Lady Patricia about addressing a great Primrose Meeting this month."

He was able, consequently, to flatter himself that he had not left a single thing unsaid which it behoved the Prime Minister to know.

Canon Spratte and Lord Stonehenge went away together. When the Canon had driven off behind a fine pair of bays, in a new and splendid brougham of the latest pattern, Lord Stonehenge lumbered into a carriage, which was both small and shabby. It was drawn by one horse only, and this was somewhat long in the tooth. There was no footman, and the coachman, in a uniform much the worse for wear, sat on his box in a slovenly, humped-up fashion. The Prime Minister and Lady Patricia drove for a while in silence; then from the depths of his beard, Lord Stonehenge summed up the party.

"They were very dull, but the dinner was eatable."

"I hope you took no ice, papa," said Lady Patricia.

"I merely tasted it," he confessed, in apologetic tones. "I wonder why we can't have ices like that. Ours are too cold."

"Lady Eastney was there, so I suppose it's not true about Sir Archibald. The Hollingtons are so careful."

"Who was she? The woman with the fat neck?"

"She sat immediately opposite Canon Spratte," answered Lady Patricia.

"Theodore Spratte wants me to make him a bishop," said Lord Stonehenge, with a slow smile.

"Well, he'll keep his clergy in order," said Lady Patricia. "He's very energetic and clever."

"I prefer them stupid," retorted the Prime Minister.

There was another pause, and presently Lord Stonehenge remembered an observation of his secretary.

"Vanhatton says I promised to do something for Spratte before the last election. I never thought we'd get in. His father was the most disagreeable man I ever saw."

"I wonder what Mr. Highbury will say to him."

"It's no business of his," retorted Lord Stonehenge, with considerable irritation.

"No, but you know what he is," answered Lady Patricia, doubtfully.

The Prime Minister meditated for some time upon the officiousness of his colleague.

"I like my bishops tedious and rather old," he said, at last. "Then their clergy give them plenty to do, and they don't meddle with the Government."

"Canon Spratte is such a staunch Conservative. He even speaks at Primrose Meetings."

"He'll only work for us as long as it pays him," said Lord Stonehenge, reflectively.

"Oh, papa, he'd never become a Radical. He's too anxious to be a gentleman."

"I prefer a Radical to a Liberal Unionist," replied the Prime Minister, with some bitterness. "I must ask Vanhatton whether I definitely committed myself."

VI

NEXT morning Canon Spratte awoke in the best of humours, and determined to chaff Lionel good-naturedly about this attachment of which he had become cognisant. He felt relieved, on the whole, that his only son had done no worse. It was much against his father's wish that the prospective heir to the peerage went into the Church, which none knew better than the Canon was no longer an eligible profession. Considering the position Lionel must one day occupy, Canon Spratte suggested that he should enter the diplomatic service or the Guards, but the boy had inherited his mother's lack of ambition rather than his father's spirit. For years the Canon had noted with irritation this timid and retiring temper. He could never understand why a man should sidle down a secluded alley when he might saunter along the sunny side of Piccadilly, and he could not help looking upon his son as something of a milksop. It would not have surprised him if Lionel had announced his desire to marry the daughter of a country clergyman. But money was more necessary than anything else to the Sprattes. The second earl had inherited all the Chancellor had to leave, and was understood never to have practised rigid economy. Theodore, finding a considerable expenditure necessary to his importance, had never been able to save a penny.

"Well, my boy, I hear that in spring a young man's fancy turns lightly to thoughts of love," he said, when Lionel bade him good-morning.

The curate looked at him with a start and reddened. Canon Spratte burst out laughing.

"A little bird has whispered to me that Master Cupid has been busy with you, Lionel. Come, come, you must have no secrets from your old father. Why have you never brought the girl to see Sophia?"

"I really don't know what you mean."

"Are you going to deny that you have cast a favourable eye upon Miss Gwendolen Durant?"

The renewal of colour upon Lionel's fair cheek assured the Canon that Mrs. Fitzherbert's surmise was eminently correct.

"I like her very much, father," admitted Lionel, after some hesitation, "but I've not said anything to her. I have no reason to believe that she cares for me at all."

"Good heavens, that's not the way to make love, my boy. Why, when I was your age I never asked if there were reasons why a young woman should care for me. It's a foolish lover who prates of his own unworthiness. If it's a fact let the lady find it out for herself after marriage."

"Would you approve of my asking Miss Durant to marry me?"

"Well, my dear Lionel, I will not conceal from you that I dislike her connection with trade, but still we live in a different world from that of my boyhood. Every one has a finger in some commercial enterprise now-a-days, and after all the Sprattes are well enough born to put up with a trifling mésalliance. I don't want you to think me cynical, but a hundred and fifty thousand pounds will gild a more tarnished scutcheon than the Durants'."

"But I've not altogether made up my mind," said Lionel, who had not bargained for being rushed into the affair.

"Well, then, make it up, my boy, for it's high time you were married. Don't forget that an old and honoured name depends on you. Your duty is to provide a male child to inherit the title, and I'm assured that the Durants run to boys."

"I'm not quite certain if I love her enough to marry her, father. I'm trying to make up my mind."

"Don't talk such nonsense, Lionel. If you don't look sharp about it, upon my soul I'll cut you out and marry her myself."

The Canon rubbed his hands and laughed heartily.

It was no wonder that his humour was jovial, for he was enjoying already his relatives' astonishment when they heard that Wroxham, most desirable of young men, wished to marry Winnie. He sent a note to his brother asking him very particularly to luncheon, but his sense of dramatic effect was far too keen to permit him even to hint that it was an occasion of peculiar solemnity.

"I shall point out to Sophia that she hasn't used her sharp eyes to very good effect," he muttered. "And if I'd depended on her to see Winnie happily married, I should have depended on a broken reed."

Had he not foreseen it since the lad was fourteen, and nourished the scheme assiduously in his paternal heart? It was a triumph for a happy father. The thought of the world's envy served nothing to decrease his complacency. The gay sunshine of May seemed to indicate that the universe at large shared and approved his self-satisfaction.

"Well, Sophia, did you see the notice about me in this morning's paper?" he cried, as he went into the drawing-room to await Wroxham's arrival.

"I've not had time to read it."

"I wish you took more interest in me!" exclaimed the Canon, not without vexation. "It's extraordinary that when there's anything in the paper, every one sees it but my own family."

"Please tell me what it is."

He took up the newspaper and with due emphasis read:

"There is no truth in the rumour that Canon Spratte, Vicar of St. Gregory's, South Kensington, has been appointed to the vacant bishopric of Barchester."

"Did you send the communication yourself, Theodore?" asked Lady Sophia, with raised eyebrows. "Surely I recognize your incisive style."

"My dear Sophia," he cried, indignantly.

But he met her calm eyes; and her dry smile of amusement called up on his own lips a smile of confession. He looked at the paragraph thoughtfully.

"I think it reads very well. It's brief, pointed, I might almost say epigrammatic; and it will certainly prevent misconception."

"Also it will remind those in power that there is no more excellent candidate than the Vicar of St. Gregory's."

"My dear Sophia, I honestly don't think any one would call me a vain man, but I cannot think myself unsuitable for the position. I'm sure you will be the last to deny that my parentage gives me certain claims upon my country."

"Which I suppose you took care to point out to Lord Stonehenge last night?"

"On the contrary, I flatter myself I was tactful enough to discuss the most indifferent matters with him. We talked of grapes and the Manager of the Army and Navy Stores. I merely remarked how sad it was that poor Andover was dead."

"Ha!"

"He agreed with me that it was very sad. For his years I thought him pleasant and intelligent. And then he talked about the General Election. I ventured to explain how important it was that the bishops should be imbued with Conservative principles."

"And d'you think he swallowed the bait?" asked Lady Sophia.

"My dear, I wish you would not express yourself quite so brutally."

"I often wonder if you humbug yourself as much as you humbug other people," she replied, with a meditative smile.

Canon Spratte stared at her with astonishment, and answered with dignity.

"Upon my soul, I don't know what you mean. I have always done my duty in that state of life in which it has pleased Providence to place me. And if I may say so without vanity, I have done it with pleasure to myself and with profit to mankind."

"Ah, yes, you're one of those men for whom the path of duty is always strewn with roses."

"It's my strength of character that makes it so," said the Canon, blandly.

"It never seems odd to you that when there are two courses open, the right one should invariably be that which redounds to your personal advantage."

"Some men, Sophia, are born to greatness; some men achieve greatness; others have greatness thrust upon them. It would be immodest in me to say which of these three more particularly applies to myself."

The answer perhaps was not very apt to the occasion, but the observation was a favourite with Canon Spratte; and he made it with such a triumphant assurance that it sounded like a very crushing retort.

"Do you remember our old nurse, Theodore?" asked Lady Sophia, smiling.

"Old Anne Ramsay?" cried Canon Spratte, in his hearty way. "To be sure I do! I shall never forget her. She was a dear old soul."

It was characteristic of him that in after years, when the nurse lived in the country on a pension, the Canon visited her with the utmost regularity. He never allowed Christmas or her birthday to pass without sending her a present. When she was attacked by a fatal illness he took a long journey to see her, by his cheerful, breezy manner did all that was possible to comfort her, and saw that she wanted nothing to make her final days easy and untroubled.

"Her affection is one of the most charming recollections of my childhood," he added.

"I always think she must have been an excellent judge of character," murmured Lady Sophia, in the even, indifferent tones she assumed when she was most sarcastic; "I remember how frequently she used to say: 'Master Theodore, self-praise is no recommendation.' "

"You certainly have the oddest memories, my dear," cried the Canon, with a scornful smile. "Now I remember how frequently she used to say: 'Miss Sophia, your nose wants blowing.' "

It was a very good hit, and Lady Sophia, bridling, answered coldly: "She was a woman of no education, Theodore."

"That is precisely what your reminiscence led me to believe," he replied, with an ironical bow.

"Humph!"

The Canon, elated by this verbal triumph, looked at her mockingly, but before Lady Sophia could find an adequate rejoinder Lord Spratte and Wroxham were shown in together. Somewhat irritated by her defeat she greeted them with relief.

To the unfortunate Wroxham, ill-at-ease and full of misgiving, luncheon seemed endless. He cursed the ingenuity of Theodore's cook, who prolonged his torture by the diversity and number of her courses. Considering with anxiety the ordeal that was before him, he found it quite impossible to join intelligently in the conversation, and feared that Winnie must think him very stupid. But Canon Spratte, tactfully realizing his condition, was as good as a band; he spoke without pause, and carried on with his brother a very lively exchange of banter. It was rarely that his family was privileged to hear so many sallies of his wit. Later, when Lady Sophia and Winnie, leaving the men to smoke, went into the drawing-room, Wroxham's nervousness became sheer agony. The affair grew intolerably grotesque when he was set at a pre-arranged hour solemnly to offer his hand and heart. Though his mind was very practical, he could not fail to see that the proceeding was excessively unromantic. He wished heartily that he had waited till he found himself by chance alone with Winnie, and could bring the conversation round by Shakespeare and the Musical Glasses to the hazardous topic of matrimony. But Canon Spratte, asking his brother and Lionel to go upstairs, led Wroxham to the study.

"I feel most awfully nervous," said the young man, doing his best to smile.

"Nonsense, my dear boy," cried the Canon, very cheerily. "There's nothing whatever to be nervous about. You have my complete assurance that Winnie undoubtedly cares for you. Now sit down quietly like a good fellow, and I'll send my little girl down to you. Bless my soul, it reminds me of the day when I asked my own dear wife to marry me."

Wroxham began to walk up and down the room, turning over in his mind what he should say. The Canon, with deliberate steps, marched to the drawing-room.

"Has Harry gone?" asked Lady Sophia.

"No, he's in my study," answered the Canon, looking down gravely.

This was the moment for which he had waited, and he paused to consider the success of his worldly wisdom.

"Dear me, how stupid I am!" he cried. "I meant to bring the paper up with me. Winnie, my love, will you fetch it for me?"

Winnie got up, but caught her father's pleased expression, and puzzled, stopped still, looking at him.

"Pray go, my dear," he added, smiling. "I left it in the study."

"But Harry is there," she said.

"I'm under the impression, my love, that he would not be sorry to have a few moments alone with you. I think he has something to say to you."

"To me, papa?" exclaimed Winnie, a little startled. "What on earth can he want?"

The Canon put his arm affectionately round her waist.

"He will tell you that himself, my love."

Winnie understood now what her father meant, and a deep blush came over her face. Then a coldness rose in her heart and travelled through every limb of her body. She was afraid and confused.

"But I can't see him, I don't want to."

She shrank away from her father; but he, somewhat amused at this resistance, led her towards the door.

"My dear, you must. I can quite understand that you should feel a certain bashfulness. But he has my full approval."

"There's something I must say to you at once, father. I want to explain."

"There's nothing to explain, my darling."

She was growing almost distracted. Her father, good-humoured and affectionate, seemed to hold her in the hollow of his hand, taking from her all strength of will.

"Father, let me speak. You don't understand."

"There's nothing to understand, my dear. I know all about it, and you really need not be nervous. You go with my very best wishes."

"I can't go. I must speak to you first," she cried desperately.

"Come, come, my dear, you must pluck up courage. It's nothing very terrible. Go downstairs like a good girl, and I daresay you'll bring Harry up with you."

He treated her as he would a child, frightened at some imaginary danger, who must be coaxed into boldness. He opened the door, and Winnie, all unwilling, yielded to his stronger mind. With a hearty laugh he came back, rubbing his hands.

"A little maidenly modesty! Very charming, very pretty! It's a lovely sight, my dear Sophia, that of the typical creamy English girl suffused in the blushes of virginal innocence."

"Fiddlesticks!" said Lady Sophia.

"You're a cynic, my dear," laughed the Canon. "It's a grave fault of which I recommend you to correct yourself."

"I beg you not to preach to me, Theodore," she answered, bridling.

"No man is a prophet in his own country," said he, with a shrug of the shoulders. Then he turned to his brother: "But you will wonder why I sent you that urgent note, asking you to luncheon."

"Not at all. I can quite understand that the pleasure of my company was worth a special messenger."

But Canon Spratte interrupted: "I asked you to come in your official capacity, if I may so call it—as the head of the family."

"My dear Theodore, merely by courtesy: I am unworthy."

"The fact is sufficiently patent without your recalling it," retorted the Canon, promptly. "But I should be obliged if at this moment, when the affairs of our house are at stake, you would adopt such sobriety and decorum as you are capable of."

"I wish I'd got my coronation robes on now," sighed Lord Spratte.

"Go on, Theodore," suggested their sister.

"Well, you will all of you be gratified to hear that Lord Wroxham has asked my permission to pay his addresses to Winnie."

"In my young days when a man wanted to marry he asked the girl before he asked her father," said Lady Sophia.

"I think it was a very proper proceeding; I am so old-fashioned as to consider a father the best judge of his daughter's welfare. And I think that in this case I am certainly the first person to be consulted. Wroxham is a young man of the very highest principles, and he naturally chose the correct course."

"And you fell upon him and said: 'What ho!' " cried Lord Spratte.

The Canon gave him a cold stare of surprise and of injured dignity.

"I informed him that I had no objection to him as a son-in-law, and I made the usual inquiries into his circumstances."

"What bloomin' cheek, when every one knows he has twenty thousand a year!"

"And finally I imparted to him my conviction that Winnie looked upon him with sincere regard."

"You are a downy old bird, Theodore," said Lord Spratte, laughing. "There's many a London matron has set her net to catch that fish."

"I did not expect that you would treat the matter with decorum, Thomas, and it was only from a strong sense of duty towards you as the head of my house, that I requested your presence."

But his elder brother was completely unabashed.

"Shut it, Theodore. You know very well that Wroxham can just about wipe his boots with the likes of us."

"I don't in the least understand what you mean," replied the Canon, frigidly. "We are his equals in the best sense; and if you wish to go into details, our rank in the peerage is—higher than his."

"Rank in the peerage be hanged! There's a deuce of a difference between the twenty-first Lord Wroxham with half a county to his back and the second Earl Spratte with a nasty pretentious stucco house and about ten acres of sooty land. Earls like us are as thick as flies."

Lady Sophia's mind, like her brother's, turned to the house which the founder of their family, on acquiring wealth, had purchased to gain the standing of a country gentleman. The Chancellor loved to get full value for his money, and its small price as well as its grandeur attracted him. Beachcombe was built by a retired ironmonger in the first years of Queen Victoria, when romance and Gothic architecture were the fashion; and it had all the appearance of a mediæval castle. With parapets, ogival windows, pointed arches, machicolations, a draw-bridge, and the other playthings of that amusing era, the grey stucco of its walls made it seem more artificial than the canvas palace of a drop-scene. The imposing hall was panelled with deal stained to resemble oak; and the walls, emblazoned with armorial bearings, gave it the gaudiness of a German beer cellar. The ceilings were coloured alternately blue and red, and decorated in gold with fleurs-de-lis and with heraldic lions. The furniture was elaborately carved, and there were settles, oak chests, and huge cabinets, on every available space of which might be seen the arms of the family of Spratte. With the best will in the world it was impossible to accept the inferior pictures, bought wholesale at an auction, as family portraits. After sixty years all this magnificence was become somewhat tawdry, and the rooms, little inhabited by their present owner, had the dismal look of a stage-set seen by daylight. The classic statues, the terraces and steps, which strove to give importance to the garden, had withstood the weather so ill that their plaster in spots was worn off and exhibited in shameful nakedness the yellow brick of which they were manufactured. The romantic grottoes were so dilapidated that they resembled kitchens burnt out and abandoned. The whole place put visibly the healthy paradox that the idealism of one age is but the vulgarity of the next.

The Canon was outraged but still dignified.

"I should like you to understand once for all, Thomas, that I very much object to the sneering manner which you are pleased to affect with regard to our family. I, for one, am proud of its origin. I am proud to be the son of the late Lord Chancellor and the grandson of a distinguished banker."

"Fiddlesticks, Theodore!" answered Lady Sophia, scornfully. "You know very well that our grandfather was a bill-broker, and rather a seedy one at that."

"He was nothing of the sort, my dear; I recollect Josiah Spratte, the elder, very well. He was a most polished and accomplished gentleman."

"My dear Theodore, you were only seven when he died. I remember only a little shabby old man who used to call my mother mam. He was always invited to dinner the day after a party to eat up the scraps, and I'm sure it never occurred to any one that he was a distinguished banker till he was safely dead and buried."

"Remember that he was my grandfather, so I should presumably know what profession he followed."

To Lady Sophia it was one of her brother's most irritating habits to assume an exclusive right to their common progenitors. Even though she was not overwhelmed by the contemplation of their greatness, she felt it hard to be altogether cut off from them.

"It's carried for bill-broking," said Lord Spratte, with a contented air. "And my belief is that the old chap did a bit of usury as well. It's no good stuffin' people, Theodore, they don't believe us."

"And what about the bill-broker's papa?" asked Lady Sophia.

"I don't believe the bill-broker had a parent at all," put in Lord Spratte. "That's where the Montmorencys come in."

"I confess I don't know what my great-grandfather was," answered Theodore, hesitating a little, "but I know he was a gentleman."

"I very much doubt it," said Lady Sophia, shaking her head. "I can't help thinking he was a green-grocer."

"Ah, that beats the Montmorencys, by Jove," cried Lord Spratte. "The ancestral green-grocer—goin' out to wait at dinner-parties in Bedford Square, and havin' a sly drink at the old sherry when no one was lookin'!"

Lady Sophia began to laugh, but the Canon looked his brother up and down, with a contemptuous twirl of his lips.

"Is this your idea of humour, Thomas?" he asked gravely, as though demanding information.

"Oh, you don't know what a load it is off my mind! Here have I been goin' about all these years with that ghastly string of Montmorencys hangin' round my neck just like the albatross and the ancient mariner, tryin' to hide from the world that I knew the family tree was bogus just as well as they did, tryin' to pretend I didn't feel ashamed of sneakin' somebody else's coat of arms. Why, I can't look at Burke without getting as red as the binding. But, by Jove, Theodore, I can live up to the ancestral green-grocer."

"I hope you will have the good sense to keep these observations from Wroxham," returned the Canon, shrugging his shoulders. "Remember that he is about to enter into an alliance with our family, and he's extremely sensitive in these matters."

"You mean he's a bit of a prig. Oh, well, he's only just come down from Oxford. He'll get over that."

"I mean nothing of the sort. I look upon him as a very excellent young man, and with his opportunities I'm convinced that he'll end up as Prime Minister."

"And suppose Winnie refuses him?" said Lord Spratte.

"What!" cried the Canon, with a jump, for such a possibility had never occurred to him. But he put it aside quickly as beyond the bounds of reason. "Nonsense! Why should she? He's a very eligible young man, and he has my full approval."

Lord Spratte shrugged his shoulders.

"Supposin' she should take it into her head to marry that Socialist Johnny? D'you know, she told me he was the handsomest man she'd ever seen in her life."

The Canon burst into a shout of laughter.

"Young Railing? Absurd! My daughter knows what is due to herself and to her family. She may be young, but she has a sense of dignity which I should be pleased to see in you, Thomas. Remember our motto: Malo mori quam fœdari, I would sooner die than be disgraced."

"I always think we were overcharged for that," murmured Lord Spratte.

"Of course a fine sentiment merely excites your ribaldry!"

"My dear Theodore, I have the receipt among the family papers."

At that moment Winnie, unhappy and pale, came quickly into the room. She gave her father a rapid look of apprehension, then, as if seeking protection, glanced appealingly at the others. But the Canon, full of complacent affection, went towards her and took her in his arms.

"My dear child!" He looked round, and with sportive tenderness gazed into his daughter's eyes. "But where is the young man? Why haven't you brought him upstairs with you, darling?"

Winnie, an expression of pain settling about her mouth, disengaged herself from the parental embrace.

"Papa, Harry has asked me to marry him."

"I know, I know. He did it with my full approval."

"I hope you won't be angry," she said, taking her father's hand, with a look of entreaty. "You wouldn't want me to do anything I didn't like, father."

"What on earth d'you mean?" he cried, surprised and uncertain.

"I had to say—that I couldn't."

The Canon started as though he were shot. "What! You're joking. Oh, it's a mistake! I won't have it. Where is he?"

He went rapidly to the door as if he meant to call back the rejected lover.

"Papa, what are you doing?" cried Winnie, distracted. "He's gone!"

The Canon stopped and came back grimly.

"I suppose you're joking, Winnie? I'm quite bewildered with all this humour."

"I don't love him, father," she said, with tearful eyes.

Canon Spratte, quite unable to comprehend, stared at her helplessly.

"The girl's mad," he cried, looking at Lady Sophia.

But Winnie felt it was no longer possible to hold back the truth. She braced herself for the contest and looked firmly into her father's eyes.

"I'm already engaged to be married, papa."

"You? And to whom, pray?"

"I'm engaged to Bertram Railing."

"Good God!"

Lady Sophia also uttered a cry of dismay, and even her uncle, though he had maliciously suggested the possibility, was no less dumfounded. In his heart he had been convinced that Winnie was far too worldly-wise to commit herself to a doubtful marriage, and he would have sworn she was incapable of a daring act. Then, against his will, the humour of the situation occurred to him, and he smothered a little laugh. But Canon Spratte, infuriated, with all his senses on the alert, divined rather than noticed this offensive merriment. He turned upon his brother angrily.

"I think we shall proceed in this matter better without your presence, Thomas," he said roughly, putting aside in his uncontrollable anger the studied urbanity upon which he prided himself. "I regret that I cannot expect from you either assistance or sympathy, or any of the feelings to be awaited in a nobleman and a gentleman. I shall be grateful if you will take your departure."

Lord Spratte smiled very good-humouredly.

"My dear Theodore, I don't want you to wash your dirty linen before me. Good-bye, Sophia."

He kissed his sister, and held out his hand to the Canon, who turned away ill-temperedly, muttering indignant things. Lord Spratte, by no means disconcerted, smiled and went up to Winnie. She was looking down, listlessly turning over the pages of a book. He put his hand kindly on her shoulder.

"Never mind, Winnie, old girl," he said, in his flippant, careless way, "you marry the man you want to, and don't be jockeyed into takin' any one else. I'll always back you up in anything unreasonable."

Winnie neither moved nor answered, but heavy tears rolled down her cheeks on to the open book.

"Well, I hope you'll all have a very nice time," said Lord Spratte. "I have the honour to wish you good-afternoon."

No one stirred till he had gone. Canon Spratte waited till the door was closed; waited, looking at his daughter, till the silence seemed intolerable.

"Now, what does all this mean, Winnie?" he asked at last.

She did not speak, and Canon Spratte tightened his lips as he watched her. You saw now for the first time the square strength of his jaw. When angry he was not a man to be trifled with, and Lady Sophia thought there was more in him at this moment of the ruthless Chancellor than she had ever known.

"Am I to understand that you are serious?"

Winnie, still looking down, nodded. The Canon stared at her for one instant, then burst out angrily with harsh tones. None would have imagined that the sonorous, sweet voice was capable of such biting inflections. But Lady Sophia could not help thinking him rather fine in his wrath.

"Oh, but you must be mad," he cried. "The child's stark, staring mad, Sophia. The whole thing is preposterous. I never heard anything like it. Do you mean seriously to tell me that you're engaged to that penniless, unknown scribbler—a man whom no one knows anything about, a rogue and a vagabond?"

But Winnie could not suffer to hear Railing ill-spoken of. The contemptuous words roused her as would have done no violence towards herself, and throwing back her head, she looked fearlessly at her father.

"You said he was a man of great intellect, papa. You said you greatly admired him."

"That proves only that I have good manners," he retorted, with a disdainful toss of his head. "When a mother shows me her baby, I say it's a beautiful child. I don't think it's a beautiful child, I think it's a very ugly child. I can't tell one baby from another, but I assure her it's the very image of its father. That's just common politeness.... How long has this absurd business been going on?"

"I became engaged to him yesterday."

Winnie, though her heart beat almost painfully, was regaining courage. The thought of Bertram strengthened her, and she was glad to fight the first battle on his behalf.

"You perceive, Sophia, that I was not consulted in this."

"Don't be ridiculous, Theodore."

Winnie took her father's hand, trying to persuade him. She felt that if it was only possible to make him comprehend how enormously the whole thing mattered to her, he would surely withdraw his opposition. He was angry because he could not see that to her it was an affair of life and death.

"Oh, don't you understand, father? You can't imagine what he's done for me. He's taught me everything I know, he's made me what I am."

"How long have you enjoyed the privilege of his acquaintance?" asked the Canon, satirically. "Six weeks?"

"I was a fool," said Winnie, speaking very quickly, with flushed cheeks. "I was just the same as any other girl, vain and empty-headed. I was happy for a week if I got a hat that became me. And then I met him and everything was changed. He found me a foolish doll, and he's made me into a woman. I'm ashamed of what I was. I'm proud now, and so grateful to him. He's the first real man I've ever known."

Canon Spratte shook his head contemptuously.

"I should like to know what you find in him that you cannot find in Wroxham or in—or in your father."

"I don't love Harry Wroxham."

"Fiddlededee! A girl of your age doesn't know what love is."

"Harry doesn't know me. He talks nonsense to me. He thinks I'm too stupid to be spoken to of serious things. To him I'm just the same as any other girl he meets at parties. For wife he wants a slave, a plaything when he's tired or bored. I want to be a man's companion. I want to work with my husband."

"I'm surprised and shocked to hear you have such ideas," answered the Canon, emphatically. "I thought you were more modest."

"You don't understand, father," cried Winnie, with despair in her voice. "Don't you see that I have a life of my own, and I must live it in my own way?"

"Rubbish! The new woman business was exploded ten years ago; you're hopelessly behind the times, my poor girl. A woman's place is in her own house. You're full of ideas which are not only silly but middle-class. They fill me with disgust. You're ridiculous, Winnie."

Canon Spratte, who only spoke the truth when he said the whole matter appeared to him suburban and vulgar, walked up and down impatiently. He sought for acid expressions of his disdain.

"You're making me dreadfully unhappy, papa," said Winnie. "You've never been unkind to me before. Think that all my happiness depends on this. You don't wish to ruin my whole life."

"Don't be absurd," cried Canon Spratte, unmoved by this entreaty. "I refuse to hear anything about it. I cannot make you marry Lord Wroxham. Far be it from me to attempt to force your affections. I confess it's a great disappointment; however, I accept it as the will of Providence and I shall do my best to bear it. But I'm quite sure it's not the will of Providence that you should marry Mr. Bertram Railing, and I utterly refuse my consent to his shameful, grotesque proposal. The man's a scoundrel; he's nothing better than a fortune-hunter."

"That's not true, father," said Winnie, flushing with anger.

"Winnie, how dare you say that!"

"You've got no right to abuse the man I love better than the whole world. Nothing you can say will make me change my mind."

"You're talking nonsense, and I think you're a very disobedient and unaffectionate girl."

"After all, it's my business alone. It's my happiness that is concerned."

"How selfish you are! You don't consider my happiness."

"I've made up my mind to marry Bertram Railing. I've given him my solemn promise."

"Women's promises are made of pie-crust," cried Canon Spratte, contemptuously.

Lady Sophia raised her eyebrows, but did not speak.

"I'm over twenty-one," retorted Winnie defiantly, for she was not without some temper of her own. "And I'm my own mistress."

"What do you mean by that, Winnie?"

"If you won't give me your consent, I shall marry without."

Canon Spratte was thunderstruck. This was rebellion, and instinctively he felt that nothing could be done with Winnie by direct contradiction. But he was too angry to devise any better way. He walked up and down indignantly.

"And this is the return I get for all the affection I have lavished upon my children," he said, speaking to no one in particular. "I've sacrificed myself to their every whim for years—and this is my reward."

Half afraid that he was beaten, Canon Spratte flung himself petulantly in a chair. As with his father before him, outspoken opposition dismayed and perhaps intimidated him; he was unused to it, and when thwarted, could not for a while think how to conduct himself. Through the conservation Lady Sophia had kept very quiet, and her calmness added to the Canon's irritation. He gave her one or two angry glances, but could hit upon nothing wherewith to vent on her his increasing choler.

"And do you know anything about this young man, Winnie?" she asked now. "Has he anything to live on?"

Winnie turned to her for comfort, thinking the worst of the struggle was over.

"We shall work hard, both of us," she said. "With what he earns and the little I have from my mother we can live like kings."

"In a flat at West Kensington, I suppose, or in a villa at Hornsey Rise," said Canon Spratte, with an angry laugh.

"With the man I love I'd live in a hovel," said Winnie, proudly.

Lady Sophia quietly smiled.

"Of course, it's a delicate question with that kind of person," she murmured. "But had he a father, or did he just grow?"

Winnie faced her wrathful parent, looking at him defiantly.

"His father is not alive. He was first-mate on a collier trading from Newcastle."

"That, I should imagine, as a profession, was neither lucrative nor clean," said Lady Sophia, in her placid way.

Canon Spratte gave a savage laugh.

"At least it's something to be thankful for that his relations are dead."

"He has a mother and a sister," said Winnie.

"And who are they, I should like to know?"

"I don't know and I don't care. He has told me already that his mother is not a very highly-educated woman."

"So I should suppose. Where do they live?"

Winnie hesitated for the very shortest moment.

"Bertram says they have a little house in—Peckham."

Canon Spratte jumped up, and an expression of real disgust passed over his face.

"Revolting!" he cried, "I wish to hear nothing more about it."

He walked towards the door, but Winnie stopped him.

"Papa, don't go. Don't be angry with me. You do love me; and I love you, next to Bertram, better than any one in the world."

Canon Spratte put aside her appealing hands.

"If you love me, Winnie, I don't know how you can cause me such pain. Sophia and I will leave you to your own reflections. I can't send you to your room as if you were a little girl, but this I must say: I think you ungrateful, disobedient, and unkind. It's only from regard to your sex, and out of respect to the memory of your dead mother, that I don't say, as well, that I consider you stupid and vulgar."

Like a martyr, for none could assume more effectively than Theodore Spratte the appearance of outraged virtue, he stalked majestically from the room.

VII

A WEEK later Canon Spratte lunched with Mrs. Fitzherbert to meet Sir John Durant and his daughter. The eminent brewer was a stout gentleman of fifty, rubicund and good-humoured, with a gold watch-chain spread widely over his capacious paunch. The few hairs that remained to him were arranged at judicious intervals over a shining pate. His face was broad and merry. His little eyes were bright with hilarity, and when anything diverted him, he laughed all over his body. He was not tall, and his legs were disproportionately short, so that the slim, elegant Canon towered over him in a way that gratified the one without mortifying the other. Sir John's appearance betokened great prosperity and a thorough satisfaction with the world at large. He knew that he made the best beer in England, and the British people knew it too, so he had good reason to be pleased with the state of things. He was a business man from top to toe, shrewd, blunt and outspoken, and he had no idea that there was anything disgraceful in his connection with trade.

When they sat down to luncheon and the butler asked if he would drink hock or claret, the brewer turned to him and in a loud, brusque voice inquired whether there was no beer.

"I always drink it to show I have confidence," he explained to the company in general. "It makes me fat, but I shouldn't be worth my salt if I hesitated at a few more pounds avoirdupois at the call of duty. I've told the British public on fifty thousand hoardings to drink Durant's Half-Crown Family Ale, and the British public do. The least they can expect of me is to follow their example."

The Canon was somewhat taken aback by the frankness with which Sir John referred to the source of his large income, but he was a man of tact, and with a laugh insisted on trying that foaming beverage.

"What d'you think of it?" asked the brewer, when Canon Spratte at one draught had emptied his glass.

"Capital, capital!"

"I'll send you some to-morrow. It's good stuff, my dear Canon—as pure as mother's milk, and it wouldn't hurt a child. I've no patience with those brewers who are ashamed of the beer they make. Why, do you know, Lord Carbis won't have it in his house, and when I stayed with him, I had to drink wine. The old fool doesn't know that people only laugh at him. However many airs he puts on, he'll never make them forget that he owes his title to stout and bitter. As far as I'm concerned, I don't mind who knows that I started as a van boy. If I've built up the biggest connection in the trade, it's to my own brains I owe it."

Mrs. Fitzherbert laughed to herself when she saw the expression with which the Canon received this statement. His idea had been that Sir John belonged to the aristocracy of beerdom, with two or even three generations of gentlemen behind him who had prepared themselves for the manufacture of fermented liquors by a career at Eton and at Oxford. It was fortunate that his cursory inspection of the brewer's daughter had been satisfactory. She was quite pretty, with a complexion whose robust colouring suggested the best of health; and her brown hair, rather abundant and waving naturally, grew low on the forehead in a way that Canon Spratte thought singularly attractive. He knew something about feminine costume, (there were few subjects of which the Canon was entirely ignorant,) and he observed with satisfaction that she was clothed with taste and fashion. He had no patience with the women who dressed in a mode they thought artistic, and he abhorred the garb which is termed rational. In a moment of expansion he had once told his daughter there were two things a woman should avoid like the seven deadly sins: she should never take her hair down and never wear a short skirt.

"A woman, like a cat, should always end in a tail," said he.

Lastly, the Canon noticed that Gwendolen Durant's handsome figure suggested that heirs would not be wanting to a union between herself and his son. This somewhat astonished him, for he would never have expected Lionel to set his affections on such a charming, but buxom, young person. He could not for the life of him imagine why she should care for Lionel.

"She's worth six of him, any day," he muttered, "though I'm his father and shouldn't think it."

But there was no accounting for taste; and if a strapping girl, with a dowry of one hundred and fifty thousand pounds, chose to make an alliance with his family, he was willing to overlook a parent who would not let an indulgent world forget his indecent connection with honest labour. Canon Spratte had that peculiar charm of manner which led people, after ten minutes' conversation, to feel they had known him all their lives; and freeing himself from the dowager, who had hitherto absorbed his attention, he turned to Miss Durant. He laid himself out to fascinate her, and they made great friends in the hour they sat side by side.

When the remaining guests had gone their ways, the Canon asked Mrs. Fitzherbert if he might stay a little longer.

"Of course," she said. "Sit down and make yourself comfortable. You may smoke a cigarette."

The day was warm and the sun shone brightly. Pale blinds kept out the brilliancy, and delicately softened the light in Mrs. Fitzherbert's drawing-room. It looked singularly restful to Canon Spratte with its gay chintzes and masses of summer flowers. It formed a fit and elegant frame for Mrs. Fitzherbert, who looked handsomer than ever in an exquisite gown, all flounces and furbelows. Its airy grace filled him with content, and he thought that feminine society was really very delightful. The world was a good place when you could sit in a pleasant drawing-room, away from the bustle of ecclesiastical labours, on a summer afternoon, and talk to an old friend who was also a fascinating woman. Yet at home there was much to make him irritable. For one thing he expected hourly a communication from the Prime Minister, offering the vacant See; and every time the bell of the street-door rang loudly, his heart leaped to his mouth. Almost unconsciously he assumed an attitude of dignified indifference, such as Cincinnatus at his plough might have used when the officers of the Republic came towards him. But Lord Stonehenge, dilatory as ever, hesitated to make an appointment. Winnie was an even greater source of annoyance. She made no sign of yielding to his wishes. She went out at all hours and none knew whither. She seemed to flaunt her legal independence in her father's indignant face. At home she was silent, frightened and sullen. Canon Spratte pointedly ignored her. He had the useful, humiliating art of looking at people without seeing them, and was able to stare at his daughter blankly as though the space she occupied were empty.

He told Mrs. Fitzherbert now the misfortune that had befallen his house, and it was a bitter confession that he had been too quick in his calculations. Mrs. Fitzherbert could not conceal a smile.

"It's really very romantic, you know. It reminds me of that poem of dear Lord Tennyson's."

"Dear Lord Tennyson hadn't a marriageable daughter," retorted the Canon, with some asperity.

"Love is so rare in this world," she hazarded, "When two young things are fond of one another, don't you think it's best to let them marry, whatever the disadvantages?"

"My dear lady, the man isn't even a gentleman."

"But we have it dinned into our ears that kind hearts are more than coronets."

"Yes, but we know very well that they're nothing of the sort," he retorted, with a laugh. "Heaven knows I'm not in the least mercenary, but I don't think any man can make my daughter happy on a penny less than two thousand a year. It's not love in a cottage, it's not love in a palace, it's just matrimony in Onslow Gardens."

He meditated for a moment or two, and slapped his knee.

"I promise you that Winnie shall break her foolish engagement with this ridiculous counter-jumper, and what's more, she shall marry Wroxham. People must get up early in the morning if they want to get the better of Theodore Spratte."

"Well, you'll need some very skilful diplomacy to achieve all that," smiled Mrs. Fitzherbert.

"The worst of it is, that though I rack my brains I can't think of any scheme that seems to promise the least measure of success."

Mrs. Fitzherbert looked at him, and her common-sense suggested to her certain obvious facts. She smiled again.

"Has Winnie seen the young man's relations yet?" she asked.

"I think not. Sophia tells me she's going down to Peckham to-morrow."

"Didn't you say that Mr. Railing's mother was the widow of a coal-heaver? I wonder what she's like."

"His sister teaches in a Board School."

"She must be an exemplary young person," answered Mrs. Fitzherbert.

"Well?"

"They must be awful. I wonder if Winnie has thought of that."

"By Jove!" cried the Canon.

The expression was not very clerical, but in his excitement he forgot the propriety of which he was usually careful. His mind was excessively alert, and Mrs. Fitzherbert's reflections, spoken almost at haphazard, gave him in a flash the plan of action he wanted. In such a manner, though with vastly less rapidity, Sir Isaac Newton is said to have discovered the theory of gravitation. The Canon's scheme was so bold that it surprised him. When he turned it over, and saw how dangerous it was, how unexpected, above all how ingeniously dramatic, he could not restrain his enthusiasm. The subtlety caught his sense of humour, and at the same time flattered his love for power. Apparently he would withdraw from the struggle, but all the time the various actors would work his will. It was well worth the risk, and he felt certain of ultimate victory. He laughed aloud, and jumping up, seized Mrs. Fitzherbert's hands.

"What a wonderful woman you are! You've saved the whole situation."

He looked at her with flaming eyes, and as she smiled upon him, he had never found her handsomer. He still held her hands.

"You know, you grow better looking each year you grow older. Upon my soul, it's not fair to the rest of us."

"Don't be so foolish," she laughed, trying to withdraw from his grasp.

"Why shouldn't I hold them?" he cried gaily. "We're old friends. Heaven knows how many years it is since first we met."

"That's just it, Heaven does know we're both of us perilously nearly fifty, and really ought to have learned how to behave by now."

"Nonsense, I won't believe a word of it. Every one knows that there is nothing so untruthful as Anno Domini, and I'm convinced that neither of us is a day more than thirty. You don't look it, and I'm sure I don't feel it."

"You really must not press my hands so hard. I tell you it's ridiculous."

She positively blushed, and the Canon's blue eyes were brighter than ever, as he noticed this sign of confusion.

"Do you remember how once we walked together in Kensington Gardens? We didn't think ourselves ridiculous then."

It was a tactless thing to say, but perhaps Theodore did not remember the exact circumstances so well as Mrs. Fitzherbert. She tightened her lips as she recalled that last scene, and there was no doubt now that she wanted him to leave her hands.

"You're hurting me," she said. "My rings."

"Oh, I'm so sorry!" He looked at her face. "But what have I said to annoy you?"

"Nothing," she replied, with a smile, recovering herself quickly. "But my carriage has been waiting for an hour, and I really must go out."

"Fool that I am! Why didn't you send me away before?"

He bent down and gallantly kissed her fingers. It is a gesture which does not come very easily to an Englishman, but Theodore Spratte carried it off with peculiar grace, and afterwards was able to leave the room without awkwardness. He was not the man to omit any of the courtesies due to the fair sex, and turned his steps immediately to a fashionable florist's, where he ordered a large bunch of red roses to be sent at once to Mrs. Fitzherbert.

"Red roses," he wrote on his card, "because they are lovely, ephemeral, and sweet smelling!"

On the way home Canon Spratte meditated upon the bold, decisive step which alone seemed capable of bringing about the ends he had in view. It was easy enough to prevent Winnie from marrying Bertram Railing; her infatuation would pass away as soon as she realized all that it entailed. But this was not enough. He knew that women may be often taken on the rebound, (perhaps his opinion of the sex was none too high,) and if he could excite a repulsion from Railing, he fancied it would lead her into the open arms of the eligible Wroxham. The Canon's classical knowledge was somewhat rusty, but he believed vaguely there was a quotation which offered apt authority for the circumstances. He could not for the moment recall it.

"Dear me!" he said, rather testily, as he put the latchkey into his front door, "my memory is certainly failing," and ironically: "It's quite time they made me a bishop."

The Canon wished to lose no time, and consequently was much pleased to find Winnie and Lady Sophia sitting by themselves in the drawing-room. It would have been inhuman to expect him to play the neat little scene without the presence of his sister. The thought of her astonishment was almost a sufficient motive for his audacious step.

"You're very pale, my dear child," he said to Winnie, "I hope you're not unwell?"

"No, father," she answered, without a smile.

"Then what is troubling you, my love? You're not yourself."

None could put into his manner such affectionate solicitude as Canon Spratte, and his voice gained such tender accents as to draw confidences from the most unwilling. Winnie sighed, but made no reply. He stroked her hair and pressed her hand.

"Come, come, my darling, you mustn't be unhappy. Nothing shall stand between you and my great affection. The only wish I have is for your welfare. Tell me frankly, is your heart still set on marrying this young man?"

Winnie looked up gravely and nodded.

"Well, well, I'm not a hard father." He smiled good-naturedly and opened his arms. "What would you say if I offered to withdraw my opposition?"

Winnie, astonished, scarcely believing her ears, sprang to her feet.

"Papa, do you mean that?"

She flung her arms round his neck and burst into tears. The Canon, pressing her to his bosom, kissed her fair hair. But Lady Sophia was dumfounded.

"Now, my dear, go to your room and wash those tears away," said he, with laughing tenderness. "You mustn't have red eyes, or people will think I'm a perfect tyrant. But mind," he shook his finger playfully as she smiled through her tears, "mind you don't put too much powder on your nose."

When Winnie was gone, Canon Spratte turned to his sister with a hearty laugh.

"The dear girl! Our children, Sophia, are often a sore trial to us, but we must take the rough with the smooth; at times also they give us a great deal of self-satisfaction."

"Did my ears deceive me?" asked Lady Sophia. "Or did you in fact consent to Winnie's preposterous engagement?"

"You're surprised, Sophia? You don't know me; you can't understand that I should sacrifice my most cherished ideas to gratify the whim of a silly school-girl. You're a clever woman, Sophia—but you're not quite so clever as your humble servant."

Lady Sophia, trying to discover what was in his mind, leaned back in her arm-chair and looked at him with keen and meditative eyes. She did not for one moment suppose that he had honestly surrendered to Winnie's obstinacy. It was her impression that Theodore was never more dangerous than when he appeared to be defeated.

"I don't understand," she confessed.

"I should have thought it was a match after your own heart," he answered, with a mocking smile. "You have always affected to look down upon our family. Surely you ought to be pleased that the descendant of your ancestral green-grocer should marry the near connection of a coal-heaver. They pair like chalk and cheese."

"Don't talk nonsense, Theodore!"

"I wonder if she calls him Bertie," murmured the Canon, thoughtfully.

"I wish to goodness you wouldn't be so irritating," said Lady Sophia, sharply. "Do you really intend Winnie to marry him?"

"Of course not, my dear. I intend Winnie to marry young Wroxham."

"And do you think the best way to bring that about is to let her be engaged to somebody else?"

"My dear Sophia, have you ever known me make a mistake yet?"

"Frequently! Though I'm bound to say I've never known you acknowledge it."

Canon Spratte laughed heartily.

"It comes to the same thing. Like the typical Englishman, I never know when I'm beaten."

"Good heavens, what a man it is!" she cried. "One can't even remark that it's a fine day without your extracting a compliment from it. Master Theodore, self-praise is no recommendation."

"Miss Sophia, your nose wants blowing," he retorted promptly.

"That I think is rather vulgar, Theodore."

Canon Spratte laughed again.

"That's just like a woman; she hits you when you're not looking, and when you defend yourself, she cries: 'Foul play!' "

"Fiddlesticks!"

There was a pause, during which Lady Sophia, knowing how anxious the Canon was to tell her about Winnie, waited for him to speak; while he, equally aware of her curiosity, determined to utter no word till she gave him the satisfaction of asking. The lady lost patience first.

"Why, then, did you consent to Winnie's engagement with the coal-heaver?" she asked, abruptly.

"Because I thought it the only way to induce her to marry Wroxham."

"Upon my word, Theodore, you're a very extraordinary man."

"That, my dear, is a fact which has not entirely escaped my observation," retorted Canon Spratte, rubbing his hands. "I've brought you to your knees, Sophia. Confess that this time your intelligence is at fault."

"Nothing of the sort!"

"Well, well, I flatter myself——" he began.

"You frequently do," interrupted his sister.

"I flatter myself that I know my daughter's character. Now, I am convinced that if I had put my foot down, Winnie would have gone off and married the man there and then. But I know the Spratte character inside and out. We are a family of marked idiosyncrasies."

"Inherited from the Montmorencys, I suppose," suggested Lady Sophia, ironically.

"I have no doubt. You will remember in our father the firmness and decision of which I speak."

"I remember that he was as obstinate as a pig."

"My dear, I do not want to rebuke you, but I really must ask you not to make these unseemly remarks. If you are incapable of recognizing the respect due to your father, I would have you recollect that he was also Lord Chancellor of England."

"Do you ever give me the chance to forget it?" murmured Lady Sophia. "But what has that to do with Winnie?"

"I was about to observe that whatever my faults, when I make up my mind that a thing is right, no power on earth can prevent me from doing it. Now, I do not wish to be offensive, but I cannot help perceiving that the firmness, which, if I may say it without vanity, is so marked a characteristic in me, is apt in other members of our family to degenerate into something which the uncharitable may well call obstinacy."

"Upon my word, Theodore, it's fortunate you told me you had no wish to be offensive."

"Please don't interrupt," pursued the Canon, with a wave of the hand. "Now, I am dealing with Winnie as the Irishman deals with the pig he is taking to market. He pulls the way he doesn't want to go, and the pig quite happily goes the other."

"I wish you'd say plainly what you're driving at."

"My dear, when Winnie said she would marry Mr. Railing, she didn't reckon on Mr. Railing's mamma and she didn't reckon on Mr. Railing's sister who teaches in the Board School. In such cases the man has often educated himself into something that passes muster, and your sex has no great skill in discerning a gentleman from the spurious article. But the women! My dear Sophia, I tell you Winnie won't like them at all."

"The more repulsive his relations are, the more her pride will force Winnie to keep her promise."

"We shall see."

Lady Sophia, pursing her lips, thought over the wily device which the Canon had complacently unfolded, then she glanced at him sharply.

"Are you quite sure it's honest, Theodore?"

"My dear Sophia, what do you mean?" cried he, much astonished.

"Isn't it a little underhand?"

Canon Spratte drew himself up and looked at his sister with some sternness.

"My dear, I do not wish to remind you that I am a clergyman, though occasionally you seem strangely oblivious of the fact. But I should like to point out to you that it's unlikely, to say the least of it, that a man of my position in the Church should do anything dishonest or underhand."

Lady Sophia, raising her eyebrows, smiled thinly.

"My dear brother, if as Vicar of St. Gregory's and Canon of Tercanbury, and prospective Bishop of Barchester, you assure me that you are acting like a Christian and a gentleman—of course I haven't the temerity to say anything further."

"You may set your mind at rest," he answered, with a little laugh of scorn, "you can be quite sure that whatever I do is right."

VIII

TWO days after this Lady Sophia was sitting alone in the drawing-room when Mrs. Fitzherbert was shown in. At her heels walked Lord Spratte.

"I found him on a chair in the Park, and I brought him here to keep him out of mischief," she said, shaking hands with Lady Sophia.

"I've reached an age when I can only get into mischief with an infinite deal of trouble," answered Lord Spratte, "and when I've succeeded, I find the game was hardly worth the candle."

"I've not seen you since Theodore turned you out of the house—somewhat unceremoniously," laughed Lady Sophia; "I hope you bear no malice."

"Not in the least; Theodore's cook is far too good."

They both talked very frankly before Mrs. Fitzherbert, whom they liked equally; but the Canon would not perhaps have been much pleased if he knew how thoroughly they discussed him in her presence. Lord Spratte asked whether there was any news of the bishopric.

"Nothing has been heard yet, but Theodore is convinced he'll get it," replied Lady Sophia.

"He'll be quite unbearable if he does."

"Quite!" she agreed. "I shall shave my head and go into a convent."

"You laugh at the Canon and you tease him, but he's a clever man for all that," said Mrs. Fitzherbert. "Of course he's rather vain and grandiloquent, but not very much more than most men. I have an idea that he'll make a first-rate bishop."

"Theodore?"

Lady Sophia considered the matter for a moment.

"It really hadn't occurred to me, but I daresay you're right," she said. "Of course he's not a saint, but one doesn't want bishops to be too pious. Curates may be saintly, and it's very proper that they should; but it's equally proper of their betters to leave them hidden away in obscure parishes where their peculiarities cannot be a stumbling-block to the faithful. The religion of a man who belongs to the Church of England is closely connected with consols, and he looks with grave distrust on the parson who tells him seriously to lay up treasure in heaven."

"A bishop must be a man who can wear his gaiters with dignity," smiled Mrs, Fitzherbert.

"But has Theodore the legs?"

"If not, he can pad," replied Lady Sophia. "Most of them do, and those that don't certainly should. A bishop must evidently be a man who can wear lawn sleeves without feeling dressed up. He's a Prince of the Church, and he should carry himself becomingly. I don't know if you've noticed it, but few of them can help purring with gratification when they hear themselves addressed by obsequious clergy as, my lord. Theodore at least will carry his honours with a dash. We may be parvenus...."

"We certainly are, Sophia," cried Lord Spratte.

"But Theodore is clever enough to forget it. He honestly feels that his ancestors fought in coats-of-mail at Agincourt and Crecy."

"Heaven save me from the candid criticism of relations," exclaimed Mrs. Fitzherbert. "They're like a bad looking-glass which gives you an atrocious squint and a crooked nose."

"We shall have to eat the dust, Sophia," muttered Lord Spratte.

"The whole diocese will have to eat the dust," she answered, smiling. "Theodore will stand no nonsense from his clergy; they'll have to do as he tells them or there'll be ructions. Theodore is not soft-handed, and he'll get his own way by hook or by crook. You'll see, in five years it'll be the best-managed bishopric in England, and an invitation to dinner at the Palace will be considered by every one a sufficient reward for the labours of Hercules."

Mrs. Fitzherbert laughed, and at that moment the subject of the conversation appeared. He greeted Mrs. Fitzherbert with extreme cordiality, but to his brother, not forgetful of the terms upon which they had parted, he held out a very frigid hand.

"I must congratulate you on Winnie's engagement," said Lord Spratte.

Canon Spratte looked at him coolly and passed his handsome hand through his hair.

"I'm sorry to see that your levity grows more marked every day, Thomas. It seems that increasing years bring you no sense of your responsibilities. I used to hope that your flippancy was due chiefly to the exuberance of youth."

"It shows what a charmin' character I have to stand bein' ragged by my younger brother," murmured Lord Spratte, calmly. He turned to Mrs. Fitzherbert. "I hate far more the relations who think it their duty to say unpleasant things to your very face."

"You forget that it's my name as well as yours that you drag through the dust."

"The name of Spratte?"

"It was held by the late Lord Chancellor of England," retorted the Canon, icily.

"Oh, Theodore, don't bring him in again. I'm just about sick of him. It's been the curse of my life to be the son of an eminent man. After all it was a beastly job that they stuck him on that silly Woolsack."

"Have you never heard the saying: 'De mortuis nil nisi bonum'?"

"That means: don't pull an old buffer's leg when he's kicked the bucket," explained Lord Spratte to the two ladies.

The Canon shrugged his shoulders.

"You have no sense of decorum, no seemliness, no dignity."

"Good heavens, what can you expect? I don't feel important enough to strike attitudes. I'm just Tommy Tiddler, and I can't forget it. I might have done something if I'd had any name but Spratte. If it had been just Sprat it would have been vulgar, but those two last letters make it pretentious as well. And that's what our honours are—vulgar and pretentious! I can't make out why the old buffer stuck to that beastly monosyllable."

"I always wish we could change with our butler, Theodore," said Lady Sophia. "Don't you think it's very hard that he should be called Ponsonby, and we—Spratte?"

"I'm not ashamed of it," said the Canon.

"You're ashamed of nothing, Theodore," retorted his brother. "Now, I'm different; I'm a modest sort of chap, and I can't stand all these gewgaws. I don't want the silly title with its sham coat-of-arms, and it's bogus pedigree. And those ridiculous ermine robes! The very thought of them makes my flesh creep. I should have been right enough if I'd just been plain Tom Sprat. I might have made a fairly good horse-dealer, and if I hadn't brains enough for that I could always have gone into Parliament. I'd have been a capital First Lord of the Admiralty, because I can't tell a man-o'-war from a coal barge, and the mere sight of the briny ocean makes me feel sick."

"It's such as you who bring the Upper House into discredit," exclaimed Theodore.

"Such as I, my dear brother? Why, I'm the saving of the place, because I have a sense of humour. I know we're no good. No one cares two straws about us. And they just leave us there because we do no harm and they've forgotten all about us."

"I should like you to compare yourself with Harry Wroxham," said Canon Spratte. "Though he's quite a young man, he has acquired a respected and assured position in the House of Lords."

"Yes, I know," replied the peer, with much scorn. "He fusses about, and he's a County Councillor, and he speaks at Church Congresses."

"It's greatly to his credit that he's a steadfast champion of the Church of England."

"I daresay. All I know is that if there were a hundred fellows in the House of Lords as enthusiastic as he is, the House of Lords would tumble down. The British public leaves us there as long as we don't interfere with it, but if ever we put on airs and try to stand on our hind legs, the British public will just take us by the scruff of the neck and out we shall go. If we all took ourselves in earnest like Wroxham, we should just get the hoof, brother Theodore."

"And do you ever go to the House of Lords, which you support by your sense of ridicule?" asked Mrs. Fitzherbert, her lips trembling into laughter.

"Certainly; I was there the other day."

"Dear me!"

"Oh, it was quite accidental," he hastened to explain, apologetically. "I had to go to Westminster on business."

"On business!" repeated the Canon, full of contempt.

"Yes, to see a terrier that a man wanted to sell. Well, I had a new topper and no umbrella, an' of course it began to rain. 'By Jove,' I said, 'I'm hanged if I won't go and legislate for ten minutes.' I saw it was only a shower. Well, I walked in and somebody asked who the dickens I was. Upon my word, I was almost ashamed to say; I look too bogus, Theodore."

"It's not the name that makes the man," said the Canon, sententiously. "A rose by any other appellation would smell as sweet."

"There you're wrong, but I won't argue it out. Well, I went in and found twenty old buffers lying about on red benches. Half of them were asleep, and one was mumblin' away in his beard. 'Good Lord,' I said, 'who are their tailors?' Then I said to myself: 'Shall I stay here and listen to their twaddle or shall I get my hat wet?' Suddenly I had an inspiration. 'By Jove,' I thought, 'I'll take a cab.' "

"And that, Sophia, is the head of our house!" said the Canon, in icy tones. "Thomas, second Earl Spratte of Beachcombe."

But these words were hardly out of his mouth, when there was a noisy ring at the bell of the front-door.

Canon Spratte started nervously. He collected himself to receive the expected messenger. Then came the sound of voices in the hall, and the Canon put up his hand to request silence.

"Who can that be?" he asked.

Some one was heard running up the stairs and the door was burst open by Lionel, for once in his life hurried and disturbed.

"Oh, it's only you!" said Canon Spratte, unable to conceal his disappointment. "I don't know why on earth you ring the bell as though the house were on fire."

But Lionel waited to make no excuses.

"I say, father, is it true about Barchester?"

"Is what true?" he asked, uncertain whether to be triumphant or dismayed.

"It's announced that Dr. Gray, the headmaster of Harbin, has been appointed."

"Impossible!" exclaimed the Canon, incredulously. "A trumpery headmaster who teaches ignorant school-boys their ABC."

"It's in the evening paper."

"Oh, it's ridiculous; it can't be true. I make the best of my fellow men, and I cannot bring myself to believe that Lord Stonehenge can be so foolish and wicked."

"The Westminster Gazette says it's a capital appointment."

"The Westminster is a Radical paper, Lionel, and will say anything. For all I know Gray may be a Radical too. I tell you it's preposterous. He's little better than an imbecile and a man of no family. A fool, a school-master! I know innumerable things against him but nothing in his favour—except that he was once tutor to one of Stonehenge's ill-mannered brats. I cannot think the Government could be so grossly idiotic as to give an important bishopric to a man of Gray's powers. Powers? They're not powers; he's the most ordinary and stupid man I've ever known. He's stupider than a churchwarden."

"I confess I think it rather bad taste of Lord Stonehenge, considering that you dined with him only the other day," murmured Lady Sophia.

"I thank Heaven that I'm not a vain man," said the Canon, somewhat oratorically. "I may have faults; we all have faults. But I don't think any one has ever accused me of vanity. When it was suggested that I should be offered the bishopric of Barchester, the thought came upon me as a surprise; but this I will confess, I don't think I should have been out of place in that position. I have been mixed up with public affairs all my life, and I am used to authority. Nor can I help thinking that I deserve something of my country."

At this moment Ponsonby passed through the drawing-room to the little terrace outside the window. He bore on a silver tray of imposing dimensions a kettle and a tea-pot.

"I told them to put tea outside," said Lady Sophia. "I thought it would be pleasanter."

Lord Spratte and Lionel got up and with Lady Sophia passed through the large French window; but Mrs, Fitzherbert, seeing that the Canon made no sign of following, stopped at the threshold.

"Won't you come and have tea, Canon?" she asked.

"Ah, my dear lady, at this moment I cannot think of tea. I could almost say that I shall never drink tea again."

"Poor Canon Spratte, I feel so sorry for you," she smiled, half amused at his vexation, half tender because he was so like a spoiled child.

He shrugged his shoulders.

"It's not for myself that I feel sorry, it's for the people who have done this thing. It's charming of you to sympathise with me." He took her hand and pressed it. "I've often felt that you really understand me. It's a dreadful thing to live surrounded by persons who don't appreciate you. They say that no man is a prophet in his own country, and I have experienced that too. I'm glad you were here this afternoon, for you've seen how I'm surrounded by cynical laughter and by flippant vulgarity. They don't understand me." He sighed and smiled and patted the hand he held. "I don't want to say anything against Sophia. I daresay she does her best, and in this world we must be thankful for small mercies, but she hasn't the delicacy of sentiment necessary to understand a character like mine. Do you remember my wife, Mrs. Fitzherbert? She was an angel, wasn't she? Loving, obedient, respectful, self-effacing! She was all that a wife should be. But she was taken from me. I shall never quite get over it."

"Now come and have tea," said Mrs. Fitzherbert, disengaging her hand. "I know it'll pull you together."

"Oh, I could touch nothing," he cried, with a gesture of distaste. "I wouldn't venture to say it to any one else, but to you who really understand me, I can say that if any man was fitted to be Bishop of Barchester I am he. Any one who knows me must be quite sure that it's not for my own sake that I wanted it; but think of the wonderful opportunities for doing good that such a position affords! And they've given it to Gray!"

He ended with a wrathful shrug of the shoulders. When he spoke again there was a tremor in his voice, partly of righteous indignation, partly of despair at the folly of mankind.

"I speak entirely without prejudice, but honestly, do you think Dr. Gray fitted for such responsibilities?"

"I certainly don't," replied Mrs. Fitzherbert, who till that day had never even heard of the distinguished pedagogue.

"I can't see that he has any claim at all. He's not a man of influence, he's not even a man of birth. Nobody ever heard of his father, while mine will be celebrated as long as English history is read."

"I can't tell you how sorry and disappointed I am."

Canon Spratte paused in his indignant promenade and waved his hand picturesquely towards the open window.

"Ah, my dear friend, don't trouble yourself with my small annoyances. Go and have tea now; it will be bad for you if you keep it standing."

"And you, dear Canon?"

"I will face the disappointment in the privacy of my own apartment."

Mrs. Fitzherbert left him, and with a despondent sigh he turned to go into his study. His glance fell on his father's portrait, and a thought came to him which in a layman might have expressed itself in the words:

"By Jove, if he were alive, he'd make 'em skip."

He shrugged his shoulders, and passing a looking-glass, paused to observe himself. Meditatively he ran his fingers through his curly, abundant hair; and then, almost without thinking what he was about, took from his pocket a little comb and passed it through the disarranged locks.

"I suppose I must go to Savile Row to-morrow, and tell them they can set to work on those trousers," he muttered.

IX

IT was almost with a sense of disillusion that Winnie realized the fight was won. Feeling very truly that opposition would only have increased her determination to marry Bertram Railing, she would have been pleased, in heroic mood, to do more desperate battle for her love. She was like a man who puts out all his strength to lift an iron weight and finds it of cardboard, light and hollow, so that he is sent sprawling on the ground. Winnie had braced herself to strenuous efforts, and since they were unneeded, the affair gained somewhat the look of a tragedy turned to farce. The conditions which the Canon had set were precise, but easy; he gave no sanction to the engagement but offered no hostility. Only, for a year nothing must be said about it to any one.

Railing was invited to luncheon at St. Gregory's Vicarage. Canon Spratte, though making no more than a passing, facetious reference to the connection with Winnie, behaved very politely. He was friendly and even cordial. The girl knew that both he and Lady Sophia examined her lover critically, and though she thought herself detestable, she could not help watching him also, nervously, in case he committed a solecism. But he was so frank, so natural, that everything he did gained a peculiar charm, and his good looks made Winnie love him each moment more devotedly. She was curious to know her aunt's opinion; but that the elderly lady took care neither by word nor manner to give, till she was asked outright.

"My dear, if you love him, and your father approves, I don't think there's anything more to be said," she smiled. "I suppose he'll go into Parliament when you're married, and I dare say it's not a bad thing that he's a Radical. The Liberals want clever young men with good connections, and doubtless your father will be able to get him made something or other."

"He wouldn't consent to be made anything," said Winnie, with scornful pride.

"After he's been married a few years he'll no doubt take anything he can get," answered Lady Sophia, mildly.

"Ah, but you don't understand, we don't want to think of ourselves, we want to think of others."

"Have you ever faced the fact that people will ask you to their parties, but won't dream of asking him?"

"D'you think I should go anywhere without my husband?"

“I’m afraid you’ll be rather bored,” suggested Lady Sophia.

Winnie reflected over this for a moment; then, chasing away a frown of indecision from her face, glanced happily at her aunt.

“At all events, you’ll allow that he’s very handsome.”

“Certainly,” said Lady Sophia. “I have only one fault to find with him. Aren’t his legs a little short? I wonder if he can wear a frock-coat without looking stumpy.”

“Fortunately, he’s absolutely indifferent to what he wears,” laughed Winnie.

“Yes, I’ve noticed that; his clothes look as if they were bought ready-made. You must really take him to a good tailor.”

Canon Spratte would much have liked to inspect Mrs. Railing and her daughter, but feared to excite Winnie’s suspicion. He contented himself with urging Bertram to take her to Peckham; and when he made the suggestion, watched the youth keenly for signs of disinclination to produce his people. He saw nothing.

“I can’t make out if the boy is simple or crafty,” he said to himself irritably.

It never struck him that Railing could have so great an affection for his mother as to be indifferent to her defects.

“She’s done everything for me,” he told Winnie, when they were in the train, on their way to visit her. “My father died when I was a lad, and it’s only by her strength of will and sheer hard work that I’ve done anything at all.”

Winnie, overflowing with love for the handsome fellow, was prepared to look upon his mother with favourable eyes. Her imagination presented to her a Roman matron, toiling with silent patience to fit her son for a great work. There was something heroic in the thought of this unassuming person, educated in the hard school of poverty, preparing with inflexible courage the instrument for the regeneration of a people. She expected to find a powerful, stern woman whom, if it was impossible to love, she might at least admire. Winnie was sure that Mrs. Railing had a thousand interesting things to say about Bertram.

“I want to know what you were like when you were a boy,” she said, in her pretty, enthusiastic way. “I want her to tell me so much.”

He kissed her fingers, in the well-made gloves, and looked at her with happy pride.

“Do you care for me really?” he asked. “Sometimes I can’t believe it. It seems too good to be true.”

Her eyes filled with tears.

“I feel so insignificant and so contemptible. I wish you knew how grateful I am to you for loving me.”

From the train they had a glimpse of the Thames glistening vaguely in the sunny mist. But they came soon to long rows of little grey houses, which displayed with callous effrontery the details of their poverty. In the grimy backyards clothes were hung out to dry on lines. Winnie, anxious to see only the more cheerful side of things, turned away to occupy herself entirely with Bertram's dark comeliness.

On reaching Peckham she looked for a cab, but her lover, to whom the idea of such luxury did not occur, set out to walk; and she, remembering that in future she must resist extravagance, dutifully followed.

"It's only about a mile and a bit," he said, stepping out briskly.

At first glance Winnie was not displeased with the bustle of the street. There was a welcome freshness in the air. The pavements were thronged, the roadway noisy with the rumble of 'buses and the clatter of tradesmen's carts; the shops were gay with all their crowded wares. After the dull respectability of South Kensington, the vivacity and the busy, strenuous eagerness were very exhilarating. The girl felt herself more in touch with humanity, and the surrounding life made her blood tingle pleasantly. She felt a singular glow as she realized what a manifold excitement there was merely in living.

"I don't think I should mind a house in the suburbs at all," she said.

But at last, turning out of the main road, they came into a street which seemed interminable. There were little brick villas on either side in a long straight row; and each house, with its bow window, its prim door and slate roof, was exactly like its fellow. Each had a tiny plot of lawn in front of it, about four feet square. The sky was grey, for the fitful sun had vanished, and the wind blew bitterly. The street, empty and cheerless, seemed very dreary. Winnie shuddered a little, feeling a sudden strange enmity towards the inhabitants of these dull places. She soon grew tired, for she was unused to walking, and asked whether they had still far to go.

"It's only just round the corner," he said.

They turned, and another long row of little houses appeared, differing not at all from the first; and the likeness between each of these made her dizzy.

"It's worse than Bayswater," she murmured, with something like a groan of dismay.

The exhilaration which at first she had felt was fast vanishing under fatigue, and the east wind, and the dull solitariness. Finally they came to a tiny villa, cheek by jowl with its neighbours, that appeared primmer, more sordid and grossly matter-of-fact than them all. Yet the name, let into the fanlight above the door, in gold letters, was its only dissimilarity. It was called Balmoral. In the windows were cheap lace curtains.

"Here we are," said Bertram, producing a latchkey.

He led her into a narrow passage, the floor of which was covered with malodorous linoleum, and then into the parlour. It was a very small room, formal, notwithstanding Bertram's books neatly arranged on shelves. There was a close smell as though it were rarely used and the windows seldom opened. A table took up most of the floor; it was hidden by a large red cloth, stamped with a black pattern, but Winnie guessed at once that its top was of deal and the legs elaborately carved in imitation mahogany. Against the wall was a piano, and all round a set of chairs covered with red velvet. On each side of the fire-place were arm-chairs of the same sort. Winnie's quick eye took in also the elaborate gilded clock with a shepherd kneeling to a shepherdess, under a glass case; and this was flanked by candlesticks to match similarly protected. The chimney-piece was swathed in pale green draperies. Opposite the looking-glass was a painting in oils of the brig Mary Ann, on which Thomas Railing had sailed many an adventurous journey; and next to this was a portrait of the seaman himself, no less wooden than the ship. He wore black broadcloth of a funereal type, and side-whiskers of great luxuriance.

"Mother," cried Bertram, "mother!"

"Coming!"

It was a fat, good-natured voice, but even in that one word the cockney accent was aggressive and unmistakable. Mrs. Railing appeared, smoothing the sleeves of the Sunday dress which she had just put on. She was a short, stout woman, of an appearance politely termed comfortable; her red face, indistinct of feature, shone with good-humour and with soap, the odour of which proceeded from her with undue distinctness; her hair was excessively black. There was certainly nothing in her to remind one of Bertram's sensitive, beautiful face. Smiling pleasantly, she shook hands with Winnie.

"Louie 'asn't come in yet, Bertie," she said, and the lacking aspirate sent a blush to Winnie's cheek. "Fine day, isn't it?" she added, by way of beginning the conversation.

Winnie agreed that it was, and Bertram suggested that they should have tea at once.

"It's all ready," said his mother.

She looked somewhat uncertainly at the bell, as though not sure whether it would be discreet to ring, and gave her son a questioning glance. Then, making up her mind, she pulled it.

The shrill sound was heard easily in the parlour, and Mrs. Railing remarked complacently: "It 'as rung."

But there was no other answer than the sound of voices in the kitchen.

"Is any one here?" asked Bertram.

"Mrs. Cooper popped in to see me, and she's been 'elpin' me get the tea ready."

Bertram's face darkened, and his mother turned to Winnie with an explanation.

"Bertie can't abide Mrs. Cooper, somehow," she said, in her voluble, good-tempered way. "You don't know Mrs. Cooper, do you? She lives in Shepherd's Bush. Such a nice woman, and a thorough lady!"

"Oh, yes," said Winnie, politely.

"But Bertie can't abide 'er. I don't deny that she does take a little drop more than's good for 'er; but she's 'ad a rare lot of trouble."

Bertram said nothing, and in an awkward pause they waited for the tea.

"I think I'd better go an' see if anything 'as 'appened," said Mrs. Railing. "We don't generally 'ave tea in here, except when we 'ave company. And that girl of mine can't be trusted to do anything unless I'm watchin' of her all the time."

But Railing rang the bell again impatiently. After a further sound of voices raised in acrimonious dispute, the door was opened about six inches, and the dishevelled head of a frowsy girl was thrust in.

"D'you want anything?"

"Do I want anything!" cried Mrs. Railing, indignantly, "I suppose you think I ring the bell for me 'ealth! I suppose I've got nothing better to do than to ring the bell all day long. Didn't I tell you to bring the tea the moment that Bertie come in?"

"Well, I'm bringing it," came from the head, crossly, and the door was closed with a bang.

"Oh, them girls!" said Mrs. Railing. "They're more trouble than they're worth, and that's the truth. The number of girls I've 'ad—well, I couldn't count 'em. They eat you out of 'ouse and 'ome, and they're always grumbling, and you 'ave to pay 'em five shillings now—they won't come for less—and they're not worth it. I 'ave to do all the work meself. And they're that particular in their eating, I never see anything like it. They must 'ave the best of everything, just the same as we 'ave, if you please."

Mrs. Railing's red face grew redder still as she described the tribulations which attend the mistress of servants.

"She broke another plate to-day, Bertie," she said. "I shall give 'er notice this week. If she stays 'ere much longer I shan't 'ave a plate in the 'ouse."

There was a knock at the door, with a clatter of cups, and Mrs. Railing opened it. A tall gaunt woman carefully brought in the tray with the tea things. She wore a bonnet and a shabby cloak, decorated with black beads.

"Oh, you've not brought it yourself, Mrs. Cooper!" cried Mrs. Railing, hastily taking the tray from her. "Why didn't you let the girl bring it? What's she here for? And I pay 'er five shillings a week."

"Oh, I thought she'd break something."

Mrs. Cooper gave Winnie an inquisitive look and turned to go.

"Now you're not going, Mrs. Cooper?"

"I know where I'm not wanted, Mrs. Railing," replied the other, with a sour glance at Bertram.

"Now don't say that, Mrs. Cooper. You don't want 'er to go, Bertie, do you?"

"I should be pleased if you'd stay and have tea, Mrs. Cooper," said Bertram, driven into a corner.

"I've 'ad 'im in me arms many a time when 'e was a baby," said Mrs. Cooper, with a defiant glare at Bertram. "An' I've bath'd 'im."

Mrs. Railing stirred the tea, put milk in each cup, and poured out.

"I 'ope you won't mind if it's not very grand," said she to Winnie, apologetically.

"Not the Queen of England could make a better cup of tea than you, Mrs. Railing," replied Mrs. Cooper, sitting down with a certain aggressiveness.

"Well, I 'ave got a silver tea-pot," said Mrs. Railing, smiling proudly. "Bertie and Louie gave it me only last week for me birthday."

Mrs. Cooper sniffed and pursed her lips.

"I don't know why you call it silver, when it's not 'all-marked, Mrs. Railing," she said.

"And I know it's not that because I've looked."

"It's electro-plate, but we call it silver by courtesy," laughed Bertram.

"I'm a woman as calls a spade a spade," answered Mrs. Cooper, with sombre dignity.

The bread was cut with the best intentions, but it was thick and plastered with slabs of butter. The tea, by way of showing hospitality, was so strong that no amount of sugar could remove the bitterness.

"I say, what a beautiful cake!" cried Bertram.

"I made it with my own 'ands," said Mrs. Railing, much gratified.

"There's no one like mother for making cakes," said Bertram, regaining his spirits, which had been damped by the appearance of Mrs. Cooper.

But this remark was taken by that lady as a deliberate slight to herself.

"You've got no cause to say that, Bertie," she remarked, bitterly. "Many's the cake you've eaten of my making in my 'ouse at Shepherd's Bush. And they was quite good enough for you then."

"You make excellent cakes too, Mrs. Cooper," he answered.

But she was not to be so easily appeased.

"I take it very 'ard that you should treat me like this, Bertie," she added, in a lachrymose way. "And you wouldn't 'ave been alive to-day if it 'adn't been for me."

"No, that you wouldn't, Bertie!" acknowledged his mother.

"I'll tell you 'ow it was," said Mrs. Cooper, turning to Winnie. "I just popped in 'ere to 'ave a little chat with Mrs. Railing, and there was Bertie in such a state—I never see anything like it. He 'ad convulsions and he was blue all over, and stiff. Oh, he was a sight, I can tell you. Well, 'e was only four months old and Mrs. Railing was in a rare state. You see, 'e was 'er first and she didn't know what to do no more than a cat would. And I said: 'It's no good sending for the doctor, Mrs. Railing,' I said, 'he'll be dead before the doctor comes. You put 'im in a 'ot bath,' I said, 'with a pinch of mustard in it.' And it saved 'is little life."

"I will say that for you, Mrs. Cooper, you do know what to do with babies," said Mrs. Railing.

"And I take it very 'ard that 'e should call me a drunken old woman," added Mrs. Cooper, putting a handkerchief to her eyes. "I've known you for thirty years, Mrs. Railing, and I ask you, 'ave you ever seen me with more than I can carry?"

"That I 'aven't, Mrs. Cooper, and you mustn't mind what Bertie says. He didn't mean to speak sharply to you."

"I beg your pardon, Mrs. Railing, and I never thought I should live to 'ear Bertie say such things to me. Last time I come 'ere, he said: 'Don't you come to my 'ouse again, Mrs. Cooper. You're a drunken old woman.' "

The tears coursed down her cheeks and she blew her nose loudly.

"And I've 'ad 'im to stay in my 'ouse at Shepherd's Bush over and over again. And I used to wash 'im meself, and comb his 'air, and I made a rare lot of 'im. I take it very 'ard that he should say I'm not to pop in and 'ave a chat with an old friend when I'm in the neighbourhood."

Bertram looked at her anxiously, afraid to speak in case there was a scene. But this apparently was just what Mrs. Cooper wanted.

"I've 'ad a very 'ard life," she said, with maudlin tears, "I've 'ad a lot of trouble with my 'usband, and I've brought up seven children—and brought them all up to earn their own living. And if I do take a little drop now and then it's because I want it. And I don't take gin like some people do."

This was obviously a home thrust, for Mrs. Railing, with a gasp, drew herself together like a war-horse panting for the fray.

"I don't know what you mean by that, Mrs. Cooper. But no one can call me a drunken old woman."

"I know all about you, Mrs. Railing. And I know a great deal more than Bertie does, and if he wants to know I'll tell him."

Mrs. Railing turned so purple that it was quite alarming.

"Oh, you're a wicked woman, Mrs. Cooper, and what your 'usband said to me only the week before last is quite true. Your 'usband 'ad something to put up with, I lay, and 'e's told me over and over again what sort of a lady you are."

"Now then, mother, for Heaven's sake don't quarrel with her now," cried Bertram.

"And what did my 'usband say to you, Mrs. Railing?"

"Never you mind, Mrs. Cooper; I'm not one to go and repeat what's been said to me privately."

Winnie had watched them with increasing alarm, and now, growing terrified, as there seemed every prospect of a battle royal, stood up.

"Bertram, it's time for me to go away."

"I'll take you to the station," he said, pale with anger.

Winnie shook hands with Bertram's mother, ruffled and hot; but pointedly ignored Mrs. Cooper. She walked past her as though no one was in the way.

When they were in the street Bertram turned to her with pleading eyes.

"I'm so sorry this has happened, darling. I had no idea that awful person would be here. My mother's the best creature in the world, but she's had a very hard time, and, like many women of that age, is inclined sometimes to drink a little more than is good for her. My sister and I are trying to get her to become a teetotaller. And Mrs. Cooper leads her on. I've told her never to come to the house, but my mother doesn't like to hurt her feelings. She made that horrible scene just to spite me, because you were here."

"It doesn't much matter, does it?" said Winnie, very wearily. "I'm not going to marry your relations."

"You're not angry with me, dearest?"

"Not at all," said Winnie, forcing a smile to her lips. "Please get me a cab; I'll drive home."

"It's too far, dearest; you must go by train. A cab would cost you a fortune."

"Well, what does it matter?" she answered, irritably. "I can afford to pay for it."

"I'm afraid there won't be one here. You see, it's so out of the world."

"Must I walk all the way along those dreary roads to the station?"

"It's not far."

They went in silence, both of them very unhappy, and Winnie angry as well, angry with herself and with all the world.

And when at length they came again to the High Street, the scene in Winnie's eye had changed its hue. The din of the traffic was insufferable to her ears, and the press of people, making it difficult to thread one's way, irritated her insanely. In their faces she saw now only a stupid mediocrity; and the petty cares which occupied them stamped their features with commonness. The gay shops were become sordid and mean. Jewellers showed silver bangles and silver brooches, low-priced and tawdry, red and green glass which masqueraded impudently under the beautiful names of emerald and ruby. Milliners offered the purchaser hats and bonnets in loud colours, imitating inexpensively what they thought the fashion of Paris. Other shops exposed the hideous details of commonplace existence, pots and pans, mangles, crockery, brushes and brooms. All things which artists had touched with their fashioning fingers, carpets, and furniture, pictures and statuettes, were cheaply parodied. Nowhere could be found restraint or modesty, but everything was flaunting and pretentious, gaudy, cheap and vulgar.

Winnie bit her lip to prevent herself from speaking, but what she wished to say was this:

"How can you talk of ideals with these people who only want

to make a show, whose needs are so ignoble and paltry? Their very faces tell you how little they care for beauty, and grace, and virtue."

At the station Bertram asked uncertainly whether she would not like him to accompany her to South Kensington.

"Please not!" she answered. "I can get home quite well alone. Will you excess my ticket?"

They had come third class, but now she wished to be in a carriage by herself. He put her in when the train came, and wistfully leaned forward.

"Won't you kiss me, dearest?"

Listlessly, with unsmiling mouth, she offered her lips. He kissed them, with eyes painfully yearning; but she, for the moment the train still lingered, kept hers averted.

"I'm so dreadfully tired," she said by way of excuse.

Quickly the guard whistled, and the train steamed away. Winnie, thankful at last to be alone, huddled into the corner as though to hide herself. She burst out weeping, passionately, hopelessly.

X

CANON SPRATTE was dispirited. Certain words which Lady Sophia had used in a discussion upon Winnie's engagement dwelt in his mind with discomforting persistence. The deliberate fashion with which she spoke gave a peculiar authority to her sayings; and though he roundly scoffed at them, the Canon could not help the feeling of uneasiness they left behind.

"After all, you can say what you like, Theodore, but in point of fact we belong to just the same class as Bertram Railing. Are you sure that Winnie is not merely sinking to our proper level? It's a tendency with families like ours, that have come up in the world; and with most of us, to keep up our nobility is just swimming against the stream."

"You're mixing your metaphors, Sophia, and I haven't an idea what you mean."

"Well, in our heart of hearts we're bourgeois, we're desperately bourgeois. But I suspect it's just the same with others as it is with us. In the last fifty years so many tinkers, tailors, and spectacle-makers have pitchforked themselves into the upper classes; and very few of them are quite at home. Some are continually on the alert to uphold their dignity, trying to hide by the stupid pretentiousness of a bogus genealogy in Burke, the grandfather who was a country attorney, or a plate-layer, or a groom. Some, with the energy still in them of all those ancestors who were honest shopkeepers or artisans, throw themselves from sheer boredom into every kind of dissipation."

"You talk like a Radical tub-thumper," said Canon Spratte, with disdain.

Lady Sophia shrugged her shoulders.

"And after all, however much they struggle, the majority, sooner or later, sink back into the ranks of the middle classes. And, once there, with what a comfortable ease they wallow!"

"Facilis descensus Averni," he murmured.

"Lord Stonehenge can make earldoms and baronies galore, but what's the good when the instincts of these new noblemen, their habits and virtues and vices, are bourgeois to the very marrow!"

Lady Sophia looked at her brother for an indignant denial of these statements, but to her surprise he answered nothing. He was very thoughtful.

"Don't you know shoals of them?" she said. "Young men who would make quite passable doctors or fairly honest lawyers, and who wear their hereditary honours like clothes several sizes too large for them? They meander through life aimlessly, like fish out of water. Look at Sir Peter Mason, whose father was President of some medical body at the Jubilee, and managed with difficulty to scrape up the needful thirty thousand pounds to accept a baronetcy. Peter was then a medical student whose ambition it was to buy a little practice in the country and marry his cousin Bertha. Well, now he's a baronet and Bertha thinks it bad form that he should drive about in a dog-cart to see patients at five shillings a visit. So they live in Essex because it's cheap, and try to keep up their dignity on a thousand a year, and they're desperately bored. Have you never met rather dowdy girls who've spent their lives in Bayswater or in some small dull terrace at South Kensington, till their father in the see-saw of politics was made a peer? How clumsily they bear their twopenny titles, how self-consciously! And with what relief they marry some obscure young man in the City!"

Canon Spratte looked at his sister for a moment, and when he answered, it was only by a visible effort that his voice remained firm.

"Sophia, if Winnie marries beneath her it will break my heart."

"Yes, you're the other sort of nouvelle noblesse, Theodore: you're the sort that's always struggling to get on equal terms with the old."

"Sophia, Sophia!"

"What do you suppose Lady Wroxham said when Harry told her he wanted to marry Winnie?"

"She's a charming woman and she has a deeply religious spirit, Sophia."

"Yes, but all the same I have an idea that she raised those thin eyebrows of hers and in that quiet, meek voice, asked: 'Winnie Spratte, Harry? Do you think the Sprattes are quite up to your form?' "

"I should think it extremely snobbish if she said anything of the sort," retorted the Canon, with all his old fire.

The conversation dropped, but he could not help it if some of these observations rankled. Lionel, on whom depended the future of the stock, proposed to marry a brewer's daughter, and Winnie was positively engaged to a man of no family. It looked indeed as though his children were sinking back into the ranks whence with so much trouble his father had emerged. Nor did the second Earl conceal his scorn for the family honours. His coronet, with the strawberry leaves and the lifted pearls, he kicked hither and thither, verbally, like a football; and the ermine cloak was a scarlet rag which never ceased to excite his derision.

"I'm the only member of the family who has a proper sense of his dignity," sighed the Canon.

But when he heard that Winnie, on her return from Peckham Rye, had gone to her room with a headache, he chased away these gloomy thoughts. Even paternal affection could not prevent him from rubbing his hands with satisfaction.

"I thought she wouldn't be very well after a visit to Mr. Railing's mamma," he said.

When she entered the drawing-room he went towards her with outstretched hands.

"Ah, my love, I see you've returned safely from the wilds of Peckham. I hope you encountered no savage beasts in those unfrequented parts."

Winnie, with a little groan of exhaustion, sank into a chair. Her head was aching still and her eyes were red with many tears. Canon Spratte assumed his most affable manner. His voice was a marvel of kindly solicitude, and only in a note here and there was perceptible a suspicion of banter.

"I hope you enjoyed yourself, my pet. You know the only wish I have in the world is to make you happy. And did your prospective mother-in-law take you to her capacious bosom?"

"She was very kind, father."

"I imagine that she was not exactly polished?"

"I didn't expect her to be," answered Winnie, in so dejected a tone that it would have melted the heart of any one less inflexible than Theodore Spratte.

"But I suppose you didn't really mind that much, did you? True disinterestedness is such a beautiful thing, and in this world, alas! so rare."

A sullen, defiant look came into Winnie's face.

"I mean to marry Bertram in spite of everything, papa."

"My darling, whoever suggested that you shouldn't? By the way, do they call him Bertie?"

"Yes, they call him Bertie."

"I thought they would," answered the Canon, with the triumphant air of a man who has found some important hypothesis verified by fact. "And Mrs. Railing's husband I think you said was connected with the sea?"

"He was first mate on a collier."

"Oh, yes. And does she smack of the briny or does she smack of Peckham Rye?"

The Canon burst into song, facetiously, with a seaman's roll, hoisting his slacks. His singing voice was melodious and full of spirit.

"For I'm no sailor bold,
And I've never been upon the sea;
And if I fall therein, it's a fact I couldn't swim,
And quickly at the bottom I should be."

He threw back his head gaily.

"My dear, how uncommunicative you are, and I'm dying with curiosity. Tell me all about Mrs. Railing. Aitchless, I presume?"

"Oh, papa, how can you, how can you!" cried Winnie, hardly keeping back the tears.

"My dear, I have no doubt they are rough diamonds, but you mustn't be discouraged at that. You must make the best of things. Remember that externals are not everything—even in this world. I'm sure the Railings are thoroughly worthy people. It is doubtless possible to eat peas with a knife, and yet to have an excellent heart. One of the most saintly women I ever knew, the old Marquise de Surennes, used invariably to wipe her knife and fork with a table-napkin before eating."

His words, notwithstanding the tone of great tenderness, were bitter stabs; and Canon Spratte, as he spoke, really could not help admiring his own cleverness.

"I should imagine that your fiancé was devoted to his mother and sister. People of that class always are. You will naturally be a good deal together. In fact, I think it probable that they will make you long and frequent visits. One's less desirable relations are such patterns of affection; they're always talking of the beauty of a united family. But I'm quite sure that you'll soon accustom yourself to their slight eccentricities of diction, to their little vulgarities of manner. Remember always that 'kind hearts are more than coronets and simple faith than Norman blood.' "

But Winnie could hold herself in no longer.

"Oh, they were awful," she cried, putting her hands to her eyes. "What shall I do? What shall I do?"

Canon Spratte, still in the swing of his rhetoric, stood in front of her. A faint smile was outlined on his lips. Was this the critical moment when the final blow might be effectively delivered? Should he suggest that it was the easiest thing in the world to break off the engagement with Bertram? He hesitated. After all, there was no need to take things hurriedly, and Providence notoriously sided with discretion and the large battalions. If Winnie suffered, it was for her good, and it was a cherished maxim with Canon Spratte that suffering was salutary. He had said in the pulpit frequently, (he was too clever a man to hesitate to repeat himself,) that the human soul was brought to its highest perfection only through distress, mental or bodily.

"Man is ennobled by pain," he said, looking so handsome that it must have been a cynic indeed who doubted that he spoke sense. "Our character is refined to pure gold. The gross lusts of the flesh, the commonness which is in all of us, the pettiness of spirit, disappear in these profitable afflictions. From a bed of sickness may spring the most delicate flowers of unselfishness, of devotion, and of true saintliness. Do not seek to avoid pain, but accept it as the surest guide to all that is in you of beauty, of heavenliness, and of truth."

For his own part, when forced to visit his dentist for the extraction of a tooth, he took good care to have gas properly administered.

In the present instance he looked upon himself as a surgeon who applies irritation that the ragged edges of an ulcer may inflame and heal. Possibly there was also in his determination to strike no sudden blow, a certain human weakness from which Canon Spratte often confessed he was not exempt. He had not the heart to interrupt the scheme which he had so ingeniously devised. He was like a debater who has convinced his adversary by the first section of an argument, but for his own pleasure, and in the interests of truth, duly exposes the rest of his contention.

He sat down at the little writing-table which was in the drawing-room and scribbled a note. He took out an envelope.

"By the way, my love, what is the address of dear Mrs. Railing?"

Winnie looked up with astonishment.

"What do you want it for?"

"Come, my darling, it's nothing improper, I hope."

"Balmoral, Rosebery Gardens, Gladstone Road."

"It sounds quite aristocratic," he said, suavely. "Their Liberalism is evidently a family tradition."

He fastened the envelope, and, blotting it, rose from the desk.

"I consider it my duty to be as cordial as possible to your future relations, Winnie, and I have a natural curiosity to make their acquaintance. I have asked Mrs. Railing to bring her daughter to tea, and I shall ask your uncle to meet them."

"Oh, father, you don't know what they're like!"

"My dear, I don't expect to find them highly educated. I take it they are rough diamonds with hearts of gold. I'm prepared to like Mrs. Railing."

"Papa, don't ask any one else—she drinks."

"Well, well, we all have our little failings in this world," returned the Canon, blandly.

He had gone too far. Winnie gave him a long, keen look, and the old note of defiance came back to her face.

"I hope you don't think I can ever break my engagement with Bertram. Nothing on earth shall induce me to do that. I've given him my solemn promise and I'd sooner die than break it."

The Canon raised his eyebrows in a very good imitation of complete amazement.

"My dear, I have not the least intention of thwarting you in any way. I think it wrong and even wicked for a father to attempt to influence his children's matrimonial choice. Their youth and inexperience naturally make them so much more capable of judging for themselves."

XI

ONE evening, to his sister's amazement, Canon Spratte volunteered to accompany Winnie to a party. The Vicar of St. Gregory's was at his best in smaller gatherings, where his personality could more easily make itself felt. He liked an attentive audience; and even one careless pair, more anxious to talk with one another than to hear his sage words, was apt to disconcert him. When he found himself in a crowd, jostled and pushed, able to speak with but one person at a time, and reduced even then to social commonplace, he quickly grew bored. He could only suffer a multitude when from the safe eminence of the pulpit, the first in place as well as in dignity of oratorial machines, he was lifted above the press of mankind. He was assured then of their attentiveness and protected from their interruption.

Winnie was very simply dressed. Her pallor was unusual, but in the soft light of shaded electricity she gained thereby a peculiar delicacy. The pose of her head was a little wearied. The blue eyes were filled with melancholy. The Canon thought her frail beauty had never been seen to greater advantage; and when, alert for all that was proceeding, he saw Wroxham coming towards them, he quickly vanished from her side. He smiled as he noticed the singular way in which the young man held his nose in the air. Wroxham was very short-sighted, and his prominent blue eyes had an odd helplessness of expression. Winnie did not see him. She was watching the throng of dancers, taking a new delight in the gaiety of those many people gathered there in lightness of heart to enjoy the fleeting moments. Never before had she found such satisfaction in the magnificence of the ball-room, hung with red roses, nor in the charming dresses of the women. She could not crush a pang that entered her breast when she thought that all this must be given up, and in sudden contrast she saw the little sordid parlour in Rosebery Gardens. Before her eyes arose the High Street at Peckham with its gaudy shops. It was hideous, hideous, and she shuddered.

Suddenly she heard in her ear a well-known voice.

"Winnie!"

Her pallor gave way before a blush that made her ten times prettier. She did not answer, but looked at Harry. In his eyes, herself quickened by suffering, she thought there was a new sadness, and a great sympathy filled her. If he lacked good looks he had at all events the kindly face of an old friend. And he was admirably dressed. Discovering for the first time that his clothes had never before attracted her attention, she observed now with what an incomparable ease he bore them. The cruel advice of Lady Sophia to get Bertram a good tailor recurred to her, and she remembered the suggestion that he could not wear a frock coat becomingly.

"I wonder if he knows it," passed through her mind. "Perhaps that's why he always wears a jacket."

It was an unwelcome thought that Bertram could be influenced by vain notions, and she upbraided herself for the pettiness of the suspicion. Wroxham, without fear of ridicule and with simplicity, could wear any clothes he chose.

"I knew I should find you here," he was saying. "You're not angry with me for coming? I wanted to see you so badly."

"Good heavens, why should I be angry?" smiled Winnie. "You have just as much right to come as I."

She could not help being flattered by the passionate love which coloured every word he spoke, and her own voice gained a sweeter tenderness.

"I can't keep away from you, Winnie. I didn't know I loved you so much."

"Oh, don't, please," she murmured, "we've been friends for ages. It would be absurd if we never saw one another again because—because of the other day. You know I'm always glad to see you."

"I couldn't take your answer as final. Oh, I don't want to bother you and make you miserable, but don't you care for me at all? Don't you think that after a time you may get to like me?"

His humility touched Winnie so much that it made her answer very difficult.

"I told you the other day it was impossible."

"Oh, I know. But then I couldn't say what I wanted. I couldn't understand. Like a fool, I thought you cared for me. I loved you so passionately that it seemed impossible I should be nothing to you at all."

"Please don't say anything more, Harry," she said, very gently. "It's awfully kind of you, and I don't know how to thank you. But I can't marry you."

Wroxham, with a little instinctive motion, set the glasses more firmly on his nose, and looked at her sadly. She smiled.

"Won't you dance with me?" she said.

His face lit up as he placed his arm round her waist and they began to waltz. The rhythm of the haunting melody carried Winnie's soul away. She knew that she was giving great happiness, and it filled her with pleasure. The music stopped, and with a sigh of delight she sank into a chair.

"I want to tell you something," he said presently, with much seriousness. "If ever you change your mind I shall be waiting for you. I can never love any one else. I don't want you to make any promise or to give me any encouragement. But I shall wait for you. And if ever the time comes that you think you can care for me, you will find me ready and eager to be—your very humble servant."

"I didn't know you were so kind," said she, with tears in her eyes. "I misjudged you, I thought you treated me like a fool. I'm sorry, I want you to be happy. But don't be wretched because I can't marry you; I'm not worth troubling about."

He looked at her fixedly, divining from her tone that something was troubling her.

"Is anything the matter?" he asked.

"No, what should be?" she answered, trying to smile, but blushing to the roots of her hair.

"You've been crying."

"I had a headache. There's really nothing else."

It was very hard to resist her impulse to confess that she was already engaged. She wished him to know why she had refused him, and wanted his loving sympathy. But at this moment a partner claimed her for the dance that was just beginning.

"Good-bye," she whispered, as she left him. "I shall never forget your kindness."

Wroxham followed her with his eyes, then, puzzled and uncertain, walked towards the door. Canon Spratte did not believe in trusting the affairs of this world to the blind hazard of chance, and it was by no accident that he found himself at this very moment in the young man's way.

"Ah, my dear fellow, I'm delighted to see you," he said. "What a crowd, isn't there? I've been dying to find some one to smoke a quiet cigarette with me."

Wroxham gave him a smile. He felt at once that cordial glow which Canon Spratte invariably suffused on all with whom he came in contact. They went to the smoking-room. Even if Wroxham had been unwilling he would have found it hard to resist the breezy authoritativeness with which the Canon, waiting for no answer, led the way.

"Now let us make ourselves at home."

He seated himself in the most comfortable arm-chair, and, for all the world as if he were in his own house, pointed Wroxham to another. In his gracious way he offered the young man a cigarette from their host's box, and having lit his own, smoked for a while in silence. He was willing to let things take their time, and waited contentedly for Wroxham to speak. He set his mind to making a number of admirable smoke rings.

"I've been talking to Winnie," said the other at last, gravely.

"Well? Well?"

"I don't understand her."

Canon Spratte put his hand impressively on Wroxham's knee.

"My dear fellow, there's nothing to understand. They say that women are incomprehensible. They're nothing of the sort. I've never met a woman that I couldn't understand at a glance."

"I fancied she'd been crying," said Wroxham, shyly.

"All women cry when they have nothing better to do. It's the only inexpensive form of amusement they have."

Wroxham knocked the ash off his cigarette with peculiar care.

"I asked her to marry me, Canon Spratte."

"And of course she refused. That was to be expected. No nice girl accepts a man the first time he proposes to her. My dear Harry, the way with women is to insist. Stand no nonsense from them. Treat them kindly, but firmly. Remember that the majority never know their own minds, and between you and me I think the majority haven't much to know."

The Canon was no feminist. It was one of his cherished convictions that women should be kept in their place, which, with regard to the lords of creation, was chiefly the background. He felt that the attitude which best became them was one of submission. Like the natural savage, unspoiled by the vice of civilization, he considered that man should hunt, fight, and be handsome, while the weaker sex toiled for the privilege of contemplating his greatness. He had never imparted these theories to Lady Sophia.

"When you want something from a woman insist upon having it," he added. "Hammer away and in the long run you'll get it."

"But Winnie is so different from other girls," replied Wroxham, unconvinced.

"Nonsense! Every man thinks the girl he wants to marry different from every other. But she's nothing of the kind. Women are very much of a muchness, especially the pretty ones. I have no patience with this ranting about the equality of the sexes. It is not only irreligious but vulgar. I lay my faith on the Bible, which tells us that women shall be subject unto man. I've never met the woman that I couldn't turn round my little finger."

He looked at that particular digit. It was adorned with a handsome ring, on which in all their monstrous fraudulence were the arms of his family. His voice rang with manly scorn.

"No, my dear Harry, you have my full approval. And you have

my assurance that Winnie undoubtedly cares for you. What more can you want? Hammer away, my dear sir, hammer away. The proper fashion to deal with a woman is to ask her in season and out of season. Propose to her morning, noon, and night. Worry her as a terrier worries a bone. Insist on marrying her. Sooner or later she'll say yes, and think herself a prodigious fool for not having done so before."

"You're very encouraging," said the lover, smiling.

Canon Spratte's cheery vigour was irresistible, and the force of his rhetoric seemed to overcome even material obstacles. But when Wroxham considered the affair he was puzzled. He was a youth of only common intelligence. This the Canon had observed with satisfaction, for he knew that nothing is so prejudicial in the world of politics as to excel the average. It did not appear natural that Winnie should refuse him out of mere virginal coyness, as the hen-bird flies from the nightingale till he has sung his most amorous lays. Her melancholy pointed to something more complex.

"You're very encouraging," he repeated, but this time with a sigh.

"There are few men who have more experience in the management of the sex than I," returned Canon Spratte, with the air of a Sultan who has conducted with unexampled success a seraglio of more than common dimensions. "Now what do you propose to do?"

"I don't know," answered Wroxham, somewhat helplessly.

"My dear fellow, God helps those who help themselves," said the Canon, with sharpness. "You want to marry my little girl and I want you to marry her. I know no one to whom I would sooner entrust her, and when a father says that, I can assure you it means a good deal."

"But what can I do?"

"Well, well, I see I must help you a little. Come and see us again in a day or two. I'll drop you a line."

"I don't want to be a bore," said Wroxham.

"I have reason to believe that you'll find Winnie in a different state of mind. Keep yourself free to come any day I fix. And now go home and have a good night's sleep."

Wroxham got up and shook hands. He left the Canon in the smoking-room. The clerical gentleman put down his cigarette and smiled to himself with much self-satisfaction. He sang again softly:

"For I'm no sailor bold,
And I've never been upon the sea;

And if I fall therein, its a fact I couldn't swim,
And quickly at the bottom I should be."

He returned to the ball-room jauntily, and on his way was so fortunate as to meet Mr. Wilson. This was the journalist of much influence in ecclesiastical circles whose good offices with the press he had already made use of.

"Ah, my dear Wilson, it was charming of you to put that little announcement in the paper for me," he said. "I'm rejoiced to see that Dr. Gray has been given the bishopric."

"I'm afraid the news is entirely premature," answered the other. "No appointment has been made at all."

"Indeed! You surprise me. It was announced so confidently in the Westminster Gazette."

"Even the newspapers are not infallible," smiled Mr. Wilson, who knew. "In point of fact, I very much doubt if Gray would accept. He's fond of the work at Harbin, and I don't think he much wants to bury himself at Barchester."

"Of course, in this world everything has its drawbacks," replied the Vicar of St. Gregory's. "And for my part, when a man is still young and vigorous, I can imagine no position with greater opportunities for good than the headmastership of a great public school."

He passed on. His name had been somewhat freely mentioned with regard to Barchester, and Canon Spratte could not bear that any one should think him disappointed or envious. He had shown Mr. Wilson that he was neither. But he could not regret that the newspapers had anticipated things; and hope, which is known to spring eternally in human breasts, cast at once a rosy hue upon the world in general. So long as no definite appointment was made, the Canon felt it only right to trust in the victory of good over evil. The various influences which he had brought to bear might still cause in Lord Stonehenge a state of mind that would raise merit to the episcopal bench.

Canon Spratte looked round the ball-room and caught sight of Gwendolen Durant. He went up to her at once. She looked uncommonly well in her low-necked dress; and the single string of pearls she wore not only showed off the youthful beauty of her neck, but reminded the world at large that she had a very opulent father.

"How is it the young men are so ungallant as to leave you sitting out?" he asked, gaily.

"I'm engaged to your son for this dance; I can't make out where he is."

“Lionel is a donkey,” laughed the Canon. “Give it to me instead.”

He would not listen to her amused objections, and in a moment they were among the dancers. Lionel came up just as Canon Spratte had borne off the prize triumphantly. He was filled with amazement, for to the best of his belief his father had not danced for twenty years. The Canon saw him, and laughing at his disconsolate look, pointed him out to Gwendolen. She laughed also.

“I’ve cut you out, dear boy,” cried the Canon as they passed, with a roguish look. “I’ve cut you out.”

“You’re very unkind,” smiled Gwendolen.

“Nonsense. It’ll teach him to be more punctual. Do you think if I’d been engaged to the belle of the evening I should have kept her waiting one single moment?”

He was so good looking, and there was about him such a buoyant charm of manner that Gwendolen was somewhat dazzled. The Canon had a great sense of rhythm, and their waltz went exceedingly well.

“You dance better than Lionel,” she said, smiling.

He pressed her hand slightly in acknowledgment of the flattering remark, and his glance positively made her heart beat a little.

“You mustn’t think because my hair is nearly white that I’m quite an old fossil.”

Gwendolen looked at his hair and thought it very handsome. She was pleased with the admiration that filled his eyes when they caught hers. She blushed, and they danced for a while in silence.

“I enjoyed that more than any dance this evening,” she sighed, when the music ceased.

“Then you must give me another. I owe you a debt of gratitude. You’ve made me feel four-and-twenty.”

“I don’t believe you’re a day more,” she answered, reddening at her boldness.

Like many young persons before her Gwendolen felt that a week’s acquaintance with Theodore Spratte had turned him into an old friend. She would have confided to him her most treasured secrets without hesitation. He took her to have an ice, and she observed with pleasure the courtliness with which he used her. It seemed more than politeness which made him so anxious for her comfort. Her wants really seemed to matter to him.

“How charmingly you wait on me,” she said, half laughing.

“I belong to the old school which put lovely women on a gilded pedestal and worshipped them. Besides, I have to take pains to make you forget my age.”

"How can you be so absurd!" she cried. "I think you're the youngest man I've ever known."

He was delighted, for he saw that Gwendolen meant precisely what she said.

"Ah, why don't we live in the eighteenth century so that I might fall on my knee and kiss your hand in gratitude for that pretty speech!"

The band struck up again, and the Canon, offering his arm, led her back to the ball-room. She was claimed by a young guardsman; and as she swung into the throng the Canon could not help feeling that neither in appearance, height, nor gallantry, had he anything to fear from the comparison.

"Upon my soul, I can't make out why I don't come to balls oftener," he murmured. "I had no idea they were so amusing."

Lionel was standing just in front of him, and he slapped him on the back.

"Well, my boy, are you enjoying yourself? I hope you bear me no malice because I robbed you of your partner."

"Not at all. I'm not really very fond of dancing."

"Ah, you young men of the present day are so superior. It's a monstrous thing that when a girl's pretty feet itch for a varnished floor she should be forced to throw herself into the arms of an old fogey like myself."

"It didn't look as if Miss Durant needed much compulsion," returned Lionel, dryly.

The Canon laughed boisterously.

"Have you declared yourself yet? She's a very nice girl indeed, and you have my paternal blessing. I think we shall get on capitally together."

"No; I haven't said anything."

"Well, my boy, why don't you? It's your duty to marry and it's your duty to marry money. You must have a son and you must have something to keep him on. I think you'll have to hunt a long time before you find any one so likely to provide all that's necessary as Gwendolen Durant."

"I like her very much," allowed Lionel, somewhat uncertainly.

"Then why don't you propose to-night? There's nothing like a dance for that sort of thing. The music and the flowers and the gaiety—it all attunes the mind to amorous affairs."

"That's all very well, but she makes one rather nervous," laughed Lionel.

"Fiddlesticks! Take her into the conservatory and play with her fan. That will lead you to take her hand. Then put your arm boldly round her waist; and the rest will follow of itself, or you're no son of mine."

Lionel shrugged his shoulders and smiled without enthusiasm.

"I see that Mrs. Fitzherbert is here," he said, inconsequently.

"Is she? I must go and find her. Take my advice, my boy; propose to Gwendolen to-night, and perhaps I'll pay a bill or two for you in the morning."

He waved his hand familiarly and disappeared in search of the handsome widow. He found her very comfortably seated in an armchair, looking at the dancers with tolerant disdain. She smiled in sympathy as she caught the happy eyes of a girl going round the room in an ecstasy of delight. She nodded with satisfaction when a handsome man passed by. She sought idly to get some notion of character as one physiognomy or another attracted her attention. But what most pleased her was the thought that she herself was merely a spectator. The delights of middle age were by no means to be despised; she was free to go where she would, sufficiently rich, indifferent to the opinion of her fellows. Twenty years ago she nearly broke her heart at a ball because she was obliged to sit out five dances running without a partner, but now her chief wish was that no one should interrupt her enjoyment of that varied scene.

Yet when Canon Spratte approached she rose to greet him with every appearance of cordiality. She wore all her diamonds and a gown whose handsome lines showed off the magnificence of her figure. He thought she had never seemed more stately.

"May I have the pleasure of a dance?" he asked, smiling, but in the most formal way.

Mrs. Fitzherbert opened her eyes wide and stared at him.

"What on earth are you talking about?"

"I don't know how I can express myself more plainly," he laughed.

"My dear Canon, I haven't danced for fifteen years."

"Come," he said gaily, "I never take a refusal. I know you dance divinely."

"Don't be so absurd! We should make ourselves perfectly ridiculous. People would roar with laughter and say: 'Look at those two old fogies doddering round together.' "

"Nothing of the sort! They'd say: 'Look at Theodore Spratte, he's dancing with the belle of the evening. Isn't that like him?' "

He put his arm round her waist, and notwithstanding a laughing remonstrance bore her into the middle of the room. It was true that he danced well, and for five minutes Mrs. Fitzherbert forgot that she was hard upon fifty. He talked the most charming nonsense. Her eyes began to flash as brightly as his, and she surrendered herself entirely to the pleasure of the waltz. It gave her a curious thrill to feel the strong hand that rested like a caress on her waist. Presently he led her into a little nook, all gay with roses, which had been arranged in an alcove on the stairs.

"You detestable creature!" she cried, sinking into a chair. "I was congratulating myself on being out of the turmoil of life, and you've made me regret it so that I could almost burst into tears."

"But acknowledge that you enjoyed it. And you know just as well as I do that you were the most beautiful woman in the room."

"How many virtuous matrons have you already assured of that fact to-night?" she asked, with a laugh.

"Ah, you think I'm joking, but I'm deadly serious," he answered.

"Then there's no possible excuse for you."

"You can't subdue me so easily as that. Does it mean nothing to you that the band is playing the most sentimental tunes and that all these roses have turned the place into a garden?"

"You see, I'm never so foolish as to forget that I'm long past forty."

"I never think of your age," he answered, and for the life of her she could not tell if he was in earnest. "To me you are a lovely woman, kind and witty and delightful."

She looked at him calmly.

"What do you think Lionel would say if he heard you talk such rubbish?"

"Lionel is wisely occupied with his own affairs. I've sent him to propose to Gwendolen Durant. He was shy, but I told him it was the simplest thing in the world. I told him to look at her fan." The Canon opened his partner's and smiled into her eyes. "And that I told him would lead him naturally to take her hand."

He audaciously seized Mrs. Fitzherbert's, but she, with a laugh, withdrew it.

"I gather your meaning without your actually giving an example," she said.

The Canon's blue eyes sparkled with all the fire of youth. Another dance had begun and they were left alone in their alcove.

"Look here, why don't you marry me?" he asked, suddenly.

Mrs. Fitzherbert was taken completely aback. It had never dawned on her that his bantering speeches could tend to any such end.

"My dear man, have you taken leave of your senses?"

"My children are making their own homes, and I shall be left alone. Whatever you say, we're neither of us old yet. Why shouldn't we join forces?"

"It's too absurd," she said.

"That I should want to marry you? Look in your glass, dear friend, and it will tell you there are a hundred good reasons."

He put his arm round her, and before she realized what he was about, kissed her lips.

"I thank you from the bottom of my heart."

"But I haven't accepted," she cried.

"I told you I never took a refusal; I shall inform Sophia that you've promised to marry me."

Giving her no time to reply, he jumped up, pressed her hand lightly, and disappeared. Mrs. Fitzherbert did not know whether to be amused or angry. The affair seemed like a joke that had been carried too far, and she really could not believe that the Canon meant what he said. Suddenly an idea struck her. A smile came to her lips and she began to laugh. The idea gained shape. She threw back her head and laughed till the tears positively ran down her cheeks.

But the Canon returned to the ball-room feeling not a day more than twenty-five. Winnie came up to him.

"I'm ready to go home when you like, papa. I'm rather tired."

He looked at his watch.

"Nonsense! One's not tired at two in the morning at your age. Why, I feel as fit as a fiddle. Come."

He seized her, and before she knew where she was, whirled her into the middle of the room. He would not let her expostulate, but danced as though he would never tire. His spirits were so high that he could have shouted at the top of his voice.

When they were all three in the carriage on their way home, Canon Spratte turned to his son.

"Well, did you take my advice?" he asked.

"I didn't have a chance," said Lionel, discontentedly.

"Good Lord! You're not half the man your father is."

The Canon chuckled and rubbed his hands. He asked Winnie's permission to light a cigar, and put up his feet comfortably on the opposite seat.

"I've had a very charming evening. Upon my soul, it's wonderful what good it does a hard-working man to have a little innocent enjoyment."

XII

MRS. RAILING accepted Canon Spratte's invitation to bring her daughter to tea. On the day appointed he sat like a Hebrew patriarch surrounded by his family and waited for her to come. He addressed Lionel, his son.

"You'll remember that there are two funerals to-morrow morning, won't you?" he said.

"Good gracious, I had completely forgotten all about them."

"I daresay they were persons of no consequence," remarked Lord Spratte.

"As a matter of fact, I believe one of them, poor fellow! was our own fish-monger," said the Canon, smiling.

"I thought the fish had been very inferior these last few days," murmured Lady Sophia.

Ponsonby opened the door stealthily and announced the guests in his most impressive tones.

"Mrs. and Miss Railing."

Mrs. Railing, a woman of simple tastes, was unaccustomed to give time or thought to the adornment of her person. She was an excellent creature who had arrived at the sensible conclusion that comfort was more important than appearance; and when she had grown used to a garment, only the repeated persuasion of her children could induce her to give it up. Widowhood with her was a question of pride and a passport to respectability. She wore, somewhat on one side, a shabby crape bonnet, a black old-fashioned cloak, and loose cotton gloves. She carried with affectionate care, as though it were a jewel of vast price, a gloomy and masculine umbrella. It had a bow on the handle.

Canon Spratte advanced very cordially and shook hands with her.

"How d'you do. How d'you do, Mrs. Railing."

"Nicely, thank you." She turned and gave a little wave of the hand toward her offspring. "This is my daughter, Miss Railing."

Miss Railing wore a strenuous look and pince-nez, a sailor hat, a white blouse, and a leather belt.

"How d'you do," said Canon Spratte.

"Quite well, thank you."

Winnie, having passed the time of day with Mrs. Railing, looked shyly at Bertram's sister.

"You weren't in the other day when I came to Peckham with your brother."

"I didn't get home till late."

Miss Railing, suffering from no false shame, looked at Winnie with a somewhat disparaging curiosity. She was highly educated and took care to speak the King's English correctly. She dropped her aitches but seldom. Sometimes she hesitated whether or no to insert the troublesome letter, but when she used it her emphasis fully made up for an occasional lapse. She was, perhaps, a little self-assertive; and came to St. Gregory's Vicarage as to an enemy's camp, bristling to take offence. She was determined to show that she was a person of culture.

"Let me introduce you to my sister, Lady Sophia Spratte," said the Canon to Mrs. Railing. "Miss Railing, my sister."

"I'm really Miss Louise Railing, you know," said that young lady, in a slightly injured tone.

"I 'ave two daughters, my lord," explained Mrs. Railing, who felt that some ceremony was needed to address the member of a noble family, "but the elder one, Florrie, ain't quite right in 'er 'ead. And we 'ad to shut 'er up in an asylum."

The Canon observed her for one moment and shot a rapid glance at Winnie.

"It's so fortunate that you were able to come," he said. "In the Season one has so many engagements."

But at the harmless remark Miss Railing bridled.

"I thought you people in the West End never did anything?"

Canon Spratte laughed heartily.

"The West End has a bad reputation—in Peckham Rye."

"Well, I don't know that I can say extra much for the people of Peckham Rye either. There's no public spirit among them. And yet we do all we can; the Radical Association tries to stir them up. We give meetings every week—but they won't come to them."

"I wonder at that," replied the Canon, blandly. "And do you share your brother's talent for oratory?"

"Oh, I say a few words now and then," said Miss Railing, modestly.

"You should hear 'er talk," interposed Mrs. Railing, with a significant nod.

"Well, I hold with women taking part in everything. I'm a Radical from top to toe." Miss Railing stared hard at Lady Sophia, who was watching her with polite attention. "I can't stand the sort of woman who sits at home and does nothing but read novels and go to balls. There's an immense field for women's activities. And who thinks now that women are inferior to men?"

"Ain't she wonderful!" ejaculated Mrs. Railing, with unconcealed admiration.

"Ma!" protested her daughter.

"She says I always praise 'er in front of people," Mrs. Railing laughed good-humouredly. "But I can't 'elp it. You should see all the prizes and certificates she's got. Oh, I am proud of 'er, I can tell you."

"Ma, don't go on like that always. It makes people think I'm a child."

"Well, Louie, I can't 'elp it. You're a marvel and there's no denying it. Tell 'em about the gold medal you won."

"I wish you would," said Lord Spratte. "I always respect people with gold medals."

"Go on with you," cried Miss Railing.

"Well, Louie, you are obstinate," said her mother; and turning to Lady Sophia she added confidentially: "She 'as been—ever since she was a child."

But the appearance of the stately Ponsonby with tea-things changed the conversation. Mrs. Railing looked round the room, and the Canon saw that her eyes rested on the magnificent portrait of the first Lord Spratte.

"That is my father, the late Lord Chancellor of England. It is a most admirable likeness."

"It's a very 'andsome frame," said Mrs. Railing, anxious to be polite.

Lord Spratte burst out laughing.

"He is plain, isn't he?"

"Oh, I didn't mean it like that," answered Mrs. Railing, with confusion, "I would never take such a liberty."

"Now, you can't honestly say he was a beauty, Mrs. Railing."

"Thomas, remember he was my father," inserted the Canon.

But Mrs. Railing feared she had wounded her host's feelings.

"Now I come to look at 'im, I don't think 'e's so bad looking after all," she said.

His elder son cast a rapid glance at the Lord Chancellor's sardonic smile.

"In the family we think he's the very image of my brother Theodore."

"Well, now you mention it, I do see a likeness," replied Mrs. Railing, innocently looking from the portrait to Canon Spratte.

The Canon shook his head at his brother with smiling menace, and handed the good lady a cup of tea. While she stirred it, she addressed herself amiably to Lady Sophia.

“Nice neighbourhood this!” she said.

“South Kensington?” answered Lady Sophia. “It’s the least unpleasant of all the suburbs.”

“My dear, I cannot allow South Kensington to be called a suburb,” cried the Canon. “It’s the very centre of London.”

Lady Sophia smiled coldly.

“It always reminds me of the Hamlet who was funny without being vulgar: South Kensington is Bayswater without being funny.”

“Peckham’s a nice neighbourhood,” said Mrs. Railing, trying to balance a piece of cake in her saucer. “You get such a nice class of people there.”

“So I should think,” replied Lady Sophia.

“We’ve got such a pretty little ’ouse near the Gladstone Road. Of course, we ’aven’t got electric light, but we’ve got a lovely bath-room. And Bertie takes a bath every morning.”

“Does he, indeed!” exclaimed the Canon.

“Yes, and ’e says he can’t do without it: if ’e doesn’t ’ave it, ’e’s uncomfortable all day. Things ’ave changed since I was a girl. Why, nobody thought of ’aving all these baths then. Now, only the other day I was talking to Mr. Smithers, the builder, an’ he said to me: ‘Lor, Mrs. Railing,’ says he, ‘people are getting that fussy, if you build ’em a house without a bath-room they won’t look at it.’ Why, even Louie takes a bath every Saturday night regular.”

“They say that cleanliness is next to godliness,” returned Canon Spratte, sententiously.

“There’s no denying that, but one ’as to be careful,” said Mrs. Railing. “I’ve known a lot of people who’ve took their death of cold all through ’aving a bath when they wasn’t feeling very well.”

Lord Spratte, giving Miss Railing a cup of tea, offered her the sugar.

“Thanks,” she said. “No sugar; I think it’s weak.”

“What, the tea?” cried the Canon. “I’m so sorry.”

“No, to take sugar. I don’t approve of hydrocarbons.”

“Rough on the hydrocarbons, ain’t it?” murmured Lord Spratte.

The Canon with a smile addressed himself again to Mrs. Railing.

“And how do you take your tea, dear lady?”

“Oh, I don’t pay no attention to all this stuff of Louie’s and Bertie’s,” that good creature replied, a broad fat smile sending her red face into a pucker of little wrinkles. “Sometimes they just about give me the ’ump, I can tell you.”

“Ma, do mind what you’re saying,” cried Miss Railing, much shocked at this manner of speaking.

"Well, you do, Louie—that is Louise. She don't like me to call her Louie. She says it's so common. You know, my lord, my children was christened Bertram and Louise. But we've always called 'em Bertie and Louie, and I can't get out of the 'abit of it now. But, lor', when your children grow up and get on in the world they want to turn everything upside down. Now what do you think Bertie wants me to do?"

"I can't imagine," said the Canon.

"Well, would you believe it, he wants me to take the pledge."

"Ma!" cried Miss Railing, with whole volumes of reproach in her tone.

"Well, look 'ere, my lord," continued her mother, confidentially. "What I say is, I'm an 'ard-working woman, and what with the work I do, I want my little drop of beer now and then. The Captain—my 'usband, that is—'ad a little bit put by, but I 'ad to work to make both ends meet when I was left a widow, I can tell you. And I've given my children a thorough good education."

"You have reason to be proud of them," replied the Canon, with conviction. "I don't suppose my little girl has half the knowledge of Miss Louise."

"That's your fault; that's because you've not educated her properly," cried Miss Railing, attacking him at once. "I hold with the higher education of women. But there's no education in the West End. Now, if I had charge of your daughter for six months I could make a different woman of her."

"Ain't she wonderful!" said Mrs. Railing. "I can listen to 'er talking for hours at a time."

"Except on the subject of teetotalism?" cried the Canon, rubbing his hands jovially.

Mrs. Railing threw back her head and shook with laughter.

"You're right there, my lord. What I say is, I'm an 'ard-working woman."

"And you want your little drop of beer, I know, I know," hastily interrupted the Canon. "I was discussing the matter the other day with the lady who does me the honour to clean out my church, and she expressed herself in the same manner; but she rather favoured spirits, I understand."

"Oh, I never take spirits," said Mrs. Railing, shaking her head.

"What, never?" cried the Canon, with immense gusto.

"Well, 'ardly ever," she answered, beaming.

"Capital! Capital!"

"Now don't you laugh at me. The fact is, I sometimes 'ave a little drop in my tea."

"Bless me, why didn't you say so? Winnie, you really ought to have told me. Ring the bell."

"Oh, I didn't mean it like that, my lord," said Mrs. Railing, who feared she had expressed too decided a hint.

"My dear lady!" cried the Canon, as though he had only just escaped a serious breach of hospitality. "What is it you take? Rum?"

"Oh, I can't bear it!" cried Mrs. Railing, throwing up both her hands and making a face.

"Whiskey?"

"Oh, no, my lord. I wouldn't touch it if I was paid."

"Gin?"

She smiled broadly and in a voice that was almost caressing, answered: "Call it white satin, my lord."

"White satin?"

"It's a funny thing now, but rum never 'as agreed with me; an' it's wholesome stuff, you know."

"I have no doubt," said Theodore, politely.

"The last time I 'ad a little drop—oh, I was queer. Now, my friend, Mrs. Cooper, can't touch anything else."

"Come, come, that's very strange."

"You don't know Mrs. Cooper, do you? Oh, she's such a nice woman. And she's got such a dear little 'ouse in Shepherd's Bush."

"A salubrious neighbourhood, I believe," said Canon Spratte, with a courteous bow.

"Oh, yes, the tube 'as made a great difference to it. You ought to know Mrs. Cooper. Oh, she's a nice woman and a thorough lady. No one can say a word against 'er, I don't care who it is!"

"Ma!" said Louise.

"Well, they do say she takes a little drop too much now and then," returned the good lady, qualifying her statement. "But I've never seen 'er with more than she could carry."

"Really!" said Canon Spratte.

"Oh, I don't approve of taking more than you can 'old. My motto is strict moderation. But as Mrs. Cooper was saying to me only the other day: 'Mrs. Railing,' she said, 'with all the trouble I've gone through, I tell you, speaking as one lady to another, I don't know what I should do without a little drop of rum.' And she 'as 'ad a rare lot of trouble. There's no denying it."

"Poor soul, poor soul!" said the Canon.

"Oh, a rare lot of trouble. Now, you know, it's funny 'ow people differ. Mrs. Cooper said to me, 'Mrs. Railing,' she said, 'I give you my word of honour, I can't touch white satin. It 'as such an effect on me that I don't know what I'm talking about.' So I said to

’er: ‘Mrs. Cooper,’ I said, ‘you’re quite right not to touch it.’ Now wasn’t I right, my lord?”

“Oh, perfectly! I think you gave her the soundest possible advice.”

At this moment Ponsonby entered the room in answer to the bell. There was in his face such an impressive solemnity that you felt it would be almost sacrilege to address him flippantly. Canon Spratte rose and stepped forward, taking, according to his habit on important occasions, as it were the centre of the stage.

“Ponsonby, have we any—white satin in the house?”

“I ’ave ’eard it called satinette,” murmured Mrs. Railing, good-humouredly.

Ponsonby’s fish-like eyes travelled slowly from the Canon to the stout lady, and he positively blinked when he saw the rakish cock of her crape bonnet. Otherwise his massive face expressed no emotion.

“White satin, sir?” he repeated, slowly. “I’ll inquire.”

“Or satinette,” added Canon Spratte, unmoved.

Ponsonby did not immediately leave the room, but looked at the Canon with a mystified expression. His master smiled quietly.

“Perhaps Ponsonby does not quite understand. I mean, have we any gin in the house, Ponsonby?”

The emotions of horror and surprise made their way deliberately from feature to feature of Ponsonby’s fleshy, immobile face.

“Gin, sir? No, sir.”

“Is there none in the servants’ hall?”

“Oh no, sir!” answered Ponsonby, scandalized into some energy of expression.

“How careless of me!” cried the Canon, with every appearance of vexation. “You ought to have reminded me that there was no gin in the house, Sophia. Well, Ponsonby, will you go and get sixpennyworth at the nearest public-house.”

“Oh no, don’t send out for it,” said Mrs. Railing, in tones of entreaty, “I could never forgive myself.”

“But I assure you it’s no trouble at all. And I should very much like to taste it.”

“Well, then, threepennyworth is ample,” answered Mrs. Railing, with a nervous glance at her daughter.

“You’re much better without it, ma,” said she.

“Come, come, you mustn’t grudge your mother a little treat now and then,” cried their host.

“And it’s a real treat for me, I can tell you,” Mrs. Railing assured him.

Canon Spratte stretched out his arm, and with a dramatic gesture pointed to the door.

"Threepennyworth of gin, Ponsonby."

"Yes, sir."

With noiseless feet Ponsonby vanished from the room. Mrs. Railing turned amiably to Lady Sophia.

"That's what I like about London, there always is a public-house round the corner."

"Ma, do mind what you're saying."

Mrs. Railing did not like these frequent interruptions, and was about to make a somewhat heated rejoinder, when Lord Spratte joined in the conversation.

"I quite agree with Mrs. Railing, I think it's most convenient."

"Oh, do you?" said Louise, aggressively. "And may I ask if you have ever studied the teetotal question?"

"Not I!"

"And you're a hereditary legislator," she answered, looking him up and down with disdain. She fixed the peer with an argumentative eye. "I should just like to have a few words with you about the House of Lords. I'm a Radical and a Home Ruler. The House of Lords must go."

"Bless you, I'll part from it without a tear."

"Now, what I want to know is what moral right have you to rule over me?"

"My dear lady, if I rule over you it is entirely unawares," replied Lord Spratte, in the most deprecating way.

Miss Railing tossed her head with an impatient gesture.

"I'm not concerned with you personally. To you as an individual I am absolutely indifferent."

"Don't say that. Why should you ruthlessly crush my self-esteem?"

"I wish to discuss the matter with you as a member of a privileged class," rejoined Miss Railing, with flashing eye, digging the ferule of her umbrella emphatically into the carpet. "Now, so far as I can see you are utterly ignorant of all the great social questions of the day."

"Utterly!" he agreed.

"What do you know about the Housing of the Working Classes?"

"Nothing!"

"What do you know about Secondary Education?"

"Nothing!"

"What do you know about the Taxation of Ground Rents?"

"Nothing!" answered Lord Spratte for the third time. "And what's more, I'm hanged if I want to."

Miss Railing sprang to her feet, waving her umbrella as though herself about to lead an attack on the Houses of Parliament.

"And yet you are a member of the Upper Chamber. Just because you're a lord, you have power to legislate over millions of people with ten times more knowledge, more ability, and more education than yourself."

"Capital! Capital!" cried Canon Spratte, vastly amused. "You rub it in. A good straight talking-to is just what he wants!"

"And how do you spend your time, I should like to know. Do you study the questions of the hour? Do you attempt to fit yourself for the task entrusted to you by the anachronism of a past age?"

"I wish you'd put that umbrella down," answered Lord Spratte. "It makes me quite nervous."

Miss Railing angrily threw that instrument of menace on a chair.

"I'll be bound you spend your days in every form of degrading pursuit. At race-meetings, and billiards, and gambling."

"Capital! Capital!" cried the Canon.

Then Ponsonby returned bearing on a silver tray, engraved magnificently with the arms and supporters of the Sprattes, a liqueur bottle.

"Ah, here is the gin!"

But Mrs. Railing had an affection for synonyms and a passion for respectability. A spasm of outraged sensibility passed over her honest face.

"Oh, my lord, don't call it gin. It sounds so vulgar. When my poor 'usband was alive I used to say to 'im: 'Captain, I won't have it called gin in my 'ouse.' I always used to call my 'usband the captain, although he was only first mate. I wish you could 'ave seen him. If any one 'ad said to me: 'Mrs. Railing, put your 'and on a fine, 'andsome, 'ealthy man,' I should 'ave put my 'and on James Samuel Railing. And would you believe it, before he was thirty-five he was no more."

"Very sad!" said the Canon.

"Oh, and 'e was a dreadful sight before 'e died. You should have seen his legs."

"Ma!"

"Leave me alone, Louie," answered Mrs. Railing, somewhat incensed. "Do you think I've never been in a gentleman's house before? You're always naggin'."

"No, I'm not, ma."

"Don't contradict, Louie. I won't 'ave it."

But Canon Spratte interposed with soft words.

"Won't you have a little more—white satin?"

"No, thank you, my lord, I don't think I could stand it," said Mrs. Railing, quickly regaining her composure. "You made the first dose rather strong, and we've got to get 'ome, you know."

"I think we ought to be trotting, ma," said her daughter.

"P'raps we ought. We've got a long way to go."

"We'd better take the train, ma."

"Oh, let's go in a 'bus, my dear," answered Mrs. Railing. "I like riding in 'buses, the conductors are so good-looking, and such gentlemen. Why, the other day I got into conversation with the conductor, and would you believe it, he made me drink a drop of beer with 'im at the end of the journey. Oh, he was a nice young man!"

"Ma!"

"Well, my dear, so 'e was. And 'e's none the worse for being a 'bus conductor. They earn very good money, and 'e told me 'e was a married man, so I don't see no 'arm in it."

"Come on, ma, or we shall never get off," said Miss Railing.

"Well, good-bye, my lord. And thank you."

Canon Spratte shook hands with them both very warmly.

"So kind of you to come all this way. We've thoroughly enjoyed your visit."

But when the door was closed behind the visitors utter silence fell upon every one in the room. Winnie looked silently in front of her, and silently Lord Spratte and Lady Sophia watched her. The Canon went to a window and glanced at the retreating figure of Mrs. Railing. He drummed on the panes and softly hummed to himself:

"For I'm no sailor bold,
And I've never been upon the sea;
And if I fell therein, it's a fact I couldn't swim,
And quickly at the bottom I should be."

Winnie got up suddenly, and without a word left the room. The Canon smiled quietly. He sat down and wrote a note to Wroxham asking him to tea on the following afternoon.

XIII

THE fates always behaved handsomely to Theodore Spratte. He was not surprised when Lady Sophia announced at luncheon next day that she meant to spend the afternoon at the Academy. The Canon expressed his regret that he would not enjoy the privilege of her society at tea, but proposed that he and Winnie should have it quite cosily by themselves. Ponsonby received private instructions that no one but Lord Wroxham should be admitted.

"And after his lordship has been here about five minutes, Ponsonby, I wish you to call me away."

When Canon Spratte gave this order he looked straight into the butler's eyes to frown down any expression of surprise; but Ponsonby replied without moving a muscle.

"Very well, sir."

He turned to leave the room, and as he did so, thinking the Canon could not see, solemnly winked at the portrait of Josiah, Lord Chancellor of England. For a moment Canon Spratte thought it must be an optical delusion, for that vast, heavy face remained impassive. Yet he would have sworn that Ponsonby's right lid descended slowly with a smooth and wary stealthiness. The Canon said no word, and when the butler at last disappeared smiled quietly to himself.

"Ponsonby is really a very remarkable character."

It was not often that Canon Spratte exerted himself when there was none but his family to admire his conversation, but on this occasion he took the greatest pains. No human being is more difficult to entertain than a young girl, and it was a clear proof of his talent that he could charm his own daughter. Winnie was listless and depressed. She shuddered still when she thought of the Railings. Their visit had precisely the effect which the Canon intended, and she was ashamed. She had seen Bertram that morning; and, perhaps owing to the sleepless night she had passed, his conversation had seemed less inspiring than usual. He was much interested in a strike which was then proceeding in Germany, and he bored her a little. One or two of his Radical theories sounded preposterous in her ears, and they had a short argument in which he proved to her that her ideas were silly and prejudiced. Once or twice Winnie had caught in his voice almost the same dictatorial manner which his sister Louise had assumed when she rated Lord Spratte. Winnie left him with a certain feeling of irritation.

But the Canon, though he knew nothing of this, took care not to refer to Railing. He drew her into a conversation on the subjects which he knew most interested her. He used every art to flatter and amuse. He told her new stories. He ridiculed comically the people he had dined with on the previous evening, and such was his gift of mimicry she could not help but laugh. His urbanity and worldly wisdom were notorious, and he had been invited to adjust some social difficulty. He now asked her advice on the point, and holding apparently an opinion contrary to hers, allowed her to convince him.

"I think there's a great deal in what you say, Winnie. It's extraordinary that the most experienced man never catches the point of such matters so accurately as a woman."

Winnie smiled with pleasure, for her father's commendation was rare enough to be valuable. Forgetting her own troubles, she enlarged upon the topic; and he, making now and then some apposite remark, listened with gratifying attention.

"Upon my word, I think you're quite right," he said at last, as though completely persuaded. "I shall do exactly as you suggest."

It was not wonderful that Winnie thought him the most remarkable of men. Then he turned to other things. He talked of his own plans and his ambitions. He knew very well that nothing compliments a young woman more than for a man of middle age to discuss with her his dearest aspirations; and Winnie felt that she had entered for the first time thoroughly into her father's life.

At length Ponsonby announced the expected visitor.

"Ah, my dear boy, I'm so pleased to see you," cried the Canon, springing to his feet with agility.

Wroxham, shyly, hesitating a little, offered his hand to Winnie.

"You must think me a dreadful bore," he said, blushing pleasantly, "I'm always coming."

"Nonsense!" interrupted his host, with great heartiness. "We're always delighted to see you. I want you to look upon the Vicarage as your second home."

Shortly afterwards, according to his orders, Ponsonby appeared again. He spoke in an undertone to the Canon, who at once got up.

"I must ask you to excuse me for a few minutes," he said, turning to Wroxham. "I have a parishioner waiting to see me—a very sad case. A poor woman who lost her husband a little while ago; and she's looking out for number two, and can't find him. A clergyman's time is never his own."

"Oh, pray don't mind me," said Wroxham.

"I shall be back in five minutes. Don't go before I see you. Winnie will do her best not to bore you."

He went out. Wroxham stepped forward to Winnie, who was pretending to alter the arrangement of flowers in a vase.

"I'm glad your father has left us alone, Winnie," he said, fixing his pince-nez more firmly. "I so seldom get a chance of speaking to you."

Winnie did not reply but pulled to pieces a marguerite.

"What does it come to?" he asked.

For a moment, not thinking of the old fancy, she made no answer; but then, remembering, held out the stalk with one remaining petal, and smiled.

"He loves me not."

"It's not true. He loves you passionately. He always will."

With a sigh Winnie threw away the flower.

"Won't you speak to me, Winnie?"

"What do you want me to say?"

He took her hand kindly, and looked into her eyes, trying to discover her thoughts, trying from sheer force of his own love, to make her tender.

"Oh, Harry, I'm so unhappy," she murmured at last. "I don't know what to do."

"Can't you love me, Winnie?" he asked, drawing her towards him. "Did you mean it when you told me never to hope?"

"I said that only a week ago, didn't I?"

"You didn't mean it?"

She tore herself from him almost violently.

"Oh, I utterly despise myself."

"But why? Why?"

She looked for a long while into his pleasant clear blue eyes, as though she sought to read his very heart.

"I wonder if you really care for me?"

"I love you with all my being," he cried, eagerly, finding in his ardent love a new eloquence. "You are all I care for in the world. You're my very life. Ah, yes, I love you with all my heart and soul."

Winnie did not answer immediately, but smiled happily. When she spoke there was in her voice the tremor of tears.

"I think I like to hear you say that."

"Ah, Winnie."

He held out his hands appealingly.

"I'm so miserable," she sighed, remembering again the events of the previous days. "I want some one so badly to care for me."

"Why don't you tell me what's the matter? I may be able to do something."

"It is kind of you to be nice to me," she smiled, almost tenderly. "You're far nicer than I ever thought you."

"Why do you torture me like this?" he cried, passionately. "Winnie, say you love me."

There was a silence. Then with a blush Winnie put her hand on his arm. A new soft look came into her eyes.

"Do you remember when I first saw you? You came here with Lionel from Eton. And you were dreadfully shy."

"But we became great friends, didn't we?"

"How angry you used to get when I beat you at tennis."

"Oh, you never did—except when I let you."

"That's what you always said, but I never believed it."

Wroxham laughed boyishly, feeling on a sudden absurdly happy. He saw that Winnie was yielding, and yet he hardly dared to think his good fortune true.

"And do you remember how I used to punt you up and down the river in the holidays?" he said.

"How frightened I was when you fell in!"

"Oh, you fibber!" he cried, with a joyful smile. "You shrieked and roared with laughter!"

Winnie, with a little laugh, turned to the sofa. Raising her eyelashes, she looked at Wroxham with the glance that she well knew set him all aflame.

"I'm so tired," she murmured.

She sat down, and he, sitting beside her, took her hand. She made no effort to withdraw it.

"What lovely days those were!" she said. "But we used to quarrel dreadfully, usen't we?"

"Only for the pleasure of making it up."

"Do you think so? You used to make me jealous by talking to other little girls."

"Oh, never!" he cried, shaking his head, firmly. "It was always you. You were so awfully flirtatious."

Winnie smiled and looked down at his hand. It held hers as though it would never again let it go.

"I wonder when you first began to like me?" she asked.

"I've never liked you. I've always loved you, passionately."

"Always? Even when I wore a pig-tail and square-toed boots?"

"Always! And I always shall," he cried, boldly putting his arm round her waist. She leaned against it as though it were a comforting support. "And I can't live without you."

"Are you sure?"

"You didn't mean it when you said you couldn't love me?" he murmured, vehemently.

She looked straight into his eyes for a moment, smiling, and slightly bent towards him.

"I don't know," she whispered.

"My dearest!"

Quickly, eagerly, he took her in his arms and kissed her lips.

"Say you'll marry me, Winnie?"

"I'll do anything to make you happy."

"Kiss me. I love you."

Blushing, she put her lips to his, and the soft pressure made him tremble with delight. He seized her hands and kissed them in passionate gratitude, repeatedly. For a while they sat in silence. Winnie, all confused, was trying to realize what she had done; but Wroxham was overwhelmed with joy.

Then the Canon's voice was heard on the stairs, singing to himself; and Winnie quickly tore herself from her lover.

"La donna è mobile," sang the Canon, coming in; "Tra-la-la-la-la Tra-la-la-la-la." He started when he saw the young couple sitting self-consciously in opposite corners of the sofa. "Hulloa, I thought you must have gone! I was detained longer than I expected."

"May I tell him?" asked Wroxham.

"Yes!"

"Canon Spratte, I want to tell you that Winnie has just promised to be my wife."

"What!" cried the Canon. "Capital! Capital! My dear fellow, I'm delighted to hear it. You know I couldn't have wanted a better son-in-law. My dear child!"

He opened his arms and Winnie hid her face on his bosom. He kissed her affectionately, and then with sincere warmth shook hands with Wroxham.

"All's well that ends well," he cried. "I knew she was devoted to you, my boy. Trust me for knowing a woman's character."

"Papa's wonderful," said Winnie, with a laugh, stretching out her hand to Wroxham.

"You've made me very happy," he said.

They discussed the situation for some time, and Canon Spratte was very bland. His wildest hopes had never led him to expect that Winnie would throw herself there and then into Wroxham's eligible arms; but an occasional glance, partly of amusement, was his only sign of surprise. The young man, promising to return for dinner, went away at last, and Theodore looked at his daughter for an explanation. She stood near a table, and began nervously to turn over the pages of a book. A smile broke on the Canon's lips, for her embarrassment told him all he wished to know.

"Would it be indiscreet to inquire when you broke off your engagement with Mr. Railing?" he asked.

Winnie looked up.

"I haven't broken it off."

"And do you intend to marry them both?"

She quickly closed the book and went up to him.

"Oh, papa, you must help me," she cried. "I'm simply distracted and I don't know what to do."

"But which of them do you propose to marry?"

"Oh, don't be unkind, father. Except for you I should never have met that man. I hate him. I'm ashamed that he ever kissed me."

"Which, my love?" he asked, as though quite perplexed. "I have every reason to believe that both embraced you."

"Papa!"

There was a pause. The Canon felt that he would be wanting in his paternal duties if he took again to his bosom a prodigal daughter without pointing out clearly the nature of her misdeeds. Some reproof, tender but dignified, gentle but explicit, was surely needed. The child had flatly disobeyed his commands.

"Do I understand that the fact that Mrs. Railing drops her aitches and drinks gin, while her daughter is bumptious and vulgar, has had any effect upon your attachment to Mr. Bertram Railing?"

"You asked them to come here, you knew what would happen," answered Winnie, flushing. "Oh, father, don't be cruel. I made a fool of myself. He took me unawares and I thought for a moment that I could live his life. But I'm frightened of him."

He said, gravely: "Which do you honestly prefer?"

For a moment she hesitated, then with a little sob replied:

"I love them both."

"I beg your pardon!" exclaimed her father, who did not in the least await such an answer.

"When I'm with one I think he's so much nicer than the other."

"Really, Winnie, you can't shilly-shally in this way," he said, considerably annoyed. "You've just told me you couldn't bear young Railing."

"I can't help it, father. When I see him I'm simply carried away. Bertram's a hero."

"Fiddlededee! He's a journalist."

"When I'm with him I'm filled with high and noble thoughts. My heart seems to grow larger so that I could throw myself at his feet. I'm not fit to be his handmaid. But I can't live up to his ideal. I have to pose all the time, and I say things I don't mean so that he may think well of me. Sometimes I'm afraid of him; I wonder what he'd say if he knew what I honestly was. He doesn't really love me, he thinks I'm full of faults. He loves his ideal and the woman I may become. He makes me feel so insignificant and so unworthy."

"And Wroxham?"

Winnie smiled happily.

"Oh, Harry's different; he loves me for myself. I can be quite natural with him, and I needn't pretend to be any better than I am. He doesn't think I have any faults and he doesn't want me any different from what I am. With Bertram I have to walk on stilts, but with Harry I can just dawdle along at my own pace, and he'll be only too glad to wait for me."

"Really, Winnie, I don't think it's quite nice for a girl of your age to analyze her feelings in this way," said the Canon, irritably. "I hate people who can't make up their minds. That is one of the few things upon which I feel justified in priding myself, that I do know my own mind."

"You will get me out of the scrape, father?"

The Canon quickly drove away all appearance of vexation, for it was evident that his daughter still required very careful handling. He took her hand and patted it affectionately.

"You see, your poor old father is still some use after all. What do you wish me to do, my child?"

"Bertram is coming here the day after to-morrow. I want you to tell him it's all a mistake and I can't marry him."

"He won't take it from me."

"Oh, he must. I daren't see him again, I should be too ashamed. But be kind to him, father. I don't want him to be unhappy."

"You need not worry yourself about that, my darling. If there's any man who can deal diplomatically with such matters I may say, without vanity, that it is I." He paused and looked at Winnie sharply. "But mind, there must be no drawing back this time, or else I leave you to get out of the muddle as best you can. Have I your full authority to tell Sophia that you're going to marry Wroxham?"

"Yes."

The Canon took her in his arms.

"Kiss me, my darling. I feel sure that you will be a credit to your father and an honour to your family."

XIV

LORD SPRATTE went to St. Gregory's Vicarage next day. His sister told him with an acid smile that he would find Theodore in the best of spirits.

"By Jove, I wonder if he'd lend me some money!" cried the head of the family. "Who's he been doin' now?"

Lady Sophia had scarcely explained when they heard the Canon come into the house. He had been out for ten minutes on some errand. This was an occasion upon which Canon Spratte felt that his fellow-creatures were very amiable. The world was an excellent place where a combination of uprightness and of pious ingenuity made the way of the virtuous not unduly hard.

On his way past the dining-room he looked in to glance at his portrait, which Orchardson had painted some fifteen years before. It was an extravagance, but when he had the chance to gratify others the Canon did not count his pence. He had been able to think of no more pleasing surprise for his wife, on the tenth anniversary of their wedding-day, than to give her a not unflattering picture of himself. He observed with satisfaction the strong lines of the hands, the open look of his blue eyes, and the bold expression of his mouth. It was a man in whose veins ran a vivacious spirit. His whole appearance was so happily self-reliant that even from the painted canvas spectators gained a feeling of exhilaration. Canon Spratte noted how well his shapely head, with the abundant fair hair, stood out against the purple background. Above, in the corner, according to his own suggestion, were the arms and the motto of his family: Malo mori quam fœdari.

"Yes, I think he did me justice," thought the Canon. "I sometimes fancy the hands are a little too large, but that may be only the perspective." He smiled to his own smiling eyes. "If I'm ever made a bishop I shall be painted again. I think it's a duty one owes one's children. I shall be painted by Sargent, in full canonicals, and I shall have an amethyst ring. It's absurd that we should habitually leave what is indeed part of the insignia of our office to a foreign Church. The English bishops have just as much right to the ring of amethyst as the bishops of the Pope. I shall have the arms of the See on the right-hand side and my own arms on the left."

He had a vivid imagination, and already saw this portrait in the Academy, on the line. It was surrounded by a crowd. Evidently it would be the picture of the year, for he felt himself capable of inspiring the painter with his own vigorous personality. He saw the country cousins and the strenuous inhabitants of Suburbia turn to their catalogues, and read: The Right Reverend the Bishop of Barchester. At the private view he saw people, recognizing him from the excellent portrait, point him out to one another. He saw his own little smile of amusement when he stood perchance for a moment in front of it, and the onlookers with rapid glance compared the original with the counterfeit. Already he marked the dashing brushwork and he fancied the painter's style suited admirably with his peculiar characteristics. He liked the shining, stiff folds of black satin, the lawn sleeves, and the delicate lace of the ruffles, the rich scarlet of his hood. He imagined the attitude of proud command which befitted a Prince of the Church, the fearless poise of the head, the firm face and the eagle eye. He would look every inch a bishop.

"How true it is that some are born to greatness!" he muttered. "I shall leave it to the National Portrait Gallery in my will."

And then, if he survived his brother, he thought with a vainglorious tremor of the describing tablet: "Theodore, 3rd Earl Spratte of Beachcombe, and Lord Bishop of Barchester."

His cheeks were flushed and his eyes sparkled, for verily he was drunk with pride. His heart beat so that it was almost painful.

With swinging step he sprang up the stairs and danced into the drawing-room like a merry West Wind. The second Earl Spratte, however, was still in the best of health.

"Ah, my dear brother, I'm delighted to see you," cried the Canon, and his voice rang like a joyous bell.

"For once in a way, Theodore. I was about to ask Sophia if you'd arranged about paddin' the gaiters yet?"

"Ha, ha, you will have your little joke, Tom." He had not used this diminutive since his brother succeeded to the title, and Lady Sophia stared at him with astonishment. "We Sprattes have always had a keen sense of humour. And what does the head of my house think of all these matrimonial schemes?"

"I've really half a mind to follow suit."

"Who is the charmer now, Thomas? Does she tread the light fantastic toe in the ballet at the Empire, or does she carol in a Gaiety chorus?"

"I have an idea that your brother Theodore is mildly facetious to-day," said the other gravely to Lady Sophia.

The Canon burst out laughing and jovially rubbed his hands.

"You must marry money, my boy."

"I would like a shot if I could. What I object to is marryin' a wife."

"One can never get money in this world without some drawback."

Lord Spratte looked at his brother with a dry smile.

"How green and yellow you'd turn, Theodore, if I did marry!"

"My dear Thomas, there's nothing that would please me more. You will do me the justice to acknowledge that I have frequently impressed upon you the desirability of marriage. I look upon it as a duty you owe to your family."

"And has the heir presumptive never in imagination fitted on his handsome head the coronet, nor draped about himself picturesquely the ermine robes? Oh, what a humbug you are, Theodore!"

"Thomas," retorted the Canon, "Thomas, how can you say such things! I can honestly say that I have never envied you. I have never allowed my mind to dwell on the possibility of surviving you."

Lord Spratte gave his brother a sharp look.

"I have led a racketty life, Theodore, and you have taken great care of yourself. There's every chance that you'll survive me. By Jupiter, you'll make things hum then!"

"I do not look upon this as a suitable matter for jesting," retorted the Canon, with suave dignity. "If Providence vouchsafes to me a longer life, you may be sure I will fulfil the duties of my rank earnestly and to the best of my ability."

"And what about the bishopric?" asked Lady Sophia.

"Who knows? Who knows?" he cried, walking about the room excitedly. "I have a presentiment that it will be offered to me."

"In that case I have a presentiment that you will accept," interrupted his brother. "You're the most ambitious man I've ever known."

"And if I am!" cried the Canon. "Ambition, says the Swan of Avon, is the last infirmity of noble minds. But what is the use of ambition now, when the Church has been wrongfully shorn of its power, and the clergy exist hazardously by sufferance of the vulgar? I should have lived four centuries ago, when the Church was a power in the land. Now it offers no scope for a man of energy. When the Tudors were kings of England a bishop might rule the country. He might be a great minister of state, holding the destinies of Europe in the hollow of his hand. I've come into the world too late. You may laugh at me, Thomas, but I tell you I feel in me the power to do great things. Sometimes I sit in my chair and I can hardly bear my inaction. Good heavens, what is there for me to do—to preach sermons to a fashionable crowd, to preside on committees, to go to dinner-parties in Mayfair. With your opportunities, Tom, I should have been Prime Minister by now, and I'd have made you Archbishop of Canterbury."

Lady Sophia looked at him, smiling. She admired the mobile mouth and the flashing eyes, as with vehement gesture he flung out his words to the indifferent air. His voice rang clear and strong.

"I tell you that I am born with the heart of a crusader," he exclaimed, striding about the room as though it were a field of battle. "In happier times I would have led the hosts of the Lord to Jerusalem. Bishops then wore coats of steel and they fought with halberd and with sword to gain the Sepulchre of the Lord their Saviour. I tell you that I cannot look at the portrait of Julius the Pope without thinking that I too have it in me to ride into action on my charger and crush the enemies of the Church. I've come into the world too late."

Lord Spratte, mildly cynical, shrugged his shoulders.

"Meanwhile you've succeeded in capturing for Winnie the best parti of the season. Talk of match-makin' mammas! They're nowhere when my brother Theodore takes the field."

"When I make up my mind to do a thing I do it."

"And what about the Socialist?"

"Oh, I think I've settled him," said the Canon, with a laugh of disdain. "What did I tell you, Sophia?"

"My dear Theodore, I have always thought you a clever man," she answered, calmly.

"I've brought you to your knees; I've humbled your pride at last. Winnie is going to marry Harry Wroxham and Lionel is nearly engaged to Gwendolen Durant. What would you say if I told you that I was going to be married too?"

They both stared at him with amazement, and he chuckled as he watched their faces.

"Are you joking, Theodore?"

"Not in the least. But I'm not going to tell you who it is yet."

"I shouldn't be surprised if it were Gwendolen," mused Lady Sophia. "Unless I'm much mistaken she's a good deal more in love with you than she is with Lionel."

"Of course one never knows, does one?" laughed the Canon. "On the other hand, it might be Mrs. Fitzherbert."

"No, I'm sure it isn't," replied Lady Sophia, with decision.

"Why?"

"Because she's a sensible woman and she'd never be such a fool as to have you."

"Wait and see, then. Wait and see."

He laughed himself out of the room, and went to his study. Here he laughed again. He had not seen Mrs. Fitzherbert since the ball, for on the following morning she had wired to say that the grave illness of a friend obliged her to go immediately into the country. The Canon had hesitated whether to write a letter; but he was prevented by his dread of ridicule from making protestations of undying affection, and knew not what else to say. He contented himself with sending a telegram:

I await your return with impatience.—Theodore.

He was dining with her that evening to meet certain persons of note. Since she had not written to postpone the party, Mrs. Fitzherbert presumably intended to return to London in the course of the day. He looked forward to the meeting with pleasurable excitement.

Canon Spratte was proud of himself. He had succeeded in all his efforts, and he felt, as men at certain times do, that he was in luck's way. He did not look upon this success as due to any fortuitous concurrence of things, but rather as a testimony to his own merit. He was vastly encouraged, and only spoke the truth when he said his presentiment was vivid, that Lord Stonehenge would offer him the Bishopric of Barchester. He was on the top of a wave, swimming bravely; and the very forces of the universe conspired to land him on an episcopal throne.

"That is how you tell what stuff a man is made of," he thought, as he tried in vain to read. "The good man has self-reliance."

He remembered with satisfaction that as soon as he heard of Bishop Andover's death, he went boldly to the tailor and countermanded the trousers he had ordered. It was a small thing, no doubt, but after all it was a clear indication of character.

St. Gregory's Vicarage stood at the corner of a square. From the study Canon Spratte could see the well-kept lawn of the garden, and the trees, dusty already in the London summer. But they seemed fresh and vernal to his enthusiastic eyes. The air blowing through the open window was very suave. Above, in the blue sky, little white clouds scampered hurriedly past, westward; and their free motion corresponded with his light, confident spirit. They too had the happy power which thrilled through every nerve of his body, and like theirs was the vigorous strength of the blood that hustled through his veins. To the careless, who believe in grim chance, it might have seemed an accident that these clouds were travelling straight to Barchester; but Canon Spratte thought that nothing in the world was purposeless. In their direction he saw an obvious and agreeable omen.

"How good life is!" he murmured. "After all, if we haven't the scope that our predecessors had, we have a great deal. The earth is always fresh and young, full of opportunity to the man who has the courage to take it."

He saw in fancy the towers and the dark roofs of Barchester. It was an old city seated in a fertile plain, surrounded by rich pasture lands and watered by smiling rivulets. He knew the pompous trees which adorned its fields and the meadows bright with buttercups. He loved the quiet streets and the gabled houses. The repose was broken only by the gay hurry of market day, when the farmers led in their cattle and their sheep: already he saw the string of horses brought in for sale, with straw plaited in their tails, and the crowd of loungers at the Corn Exchange. Above all, his fancy lingered among the grey stones of the cathedral, with its lofty nave; and in the close with the ancient elms and the careful, sweet-smelling lawns. He thought of the rich service, the imposing procession of the clergy, and the magnificent throne carved by sculptors long forgotten, in which himself would sit so proudly.

"Oh, yes, the world is very good!" he cried.

He was so immersed in thought that he did not hear Ponsonby come into the room, and started violently when he heard a voice behind him.

"This letter has just come for you, sir."

He knew at once that it was from Lord Stonehenge. The certainty came to him with the force of an inspiration, and his heart beat violently.

"Very well," he said. "Put it on my desk."

He turned pale, but did not move till the servant was gone. He took it with shaking hands. He was right, for he recognized the official paper. At last! For some time he looked at the envelope, but trembled so much that he could not open it. He grew sick with expectation and his brain throbbed as if he would faint. A feeling of thankfulness came into his heart. Now the cup of his desire was filled. He held his head for a moment and breathed deeply, then slowly cut open the envelope. With habitual neatness he used a paper-knife.

Dear Canon Spratte,

It is my desire, if it meet your own wishes, to recommend His

Majesty to appoint you to the Deanery of St. Olphert's, vacant through the impending retirement from illness of Dr. Tanner. In so doing, I can assure you I feel great pleasure in being able to mark my appreciation of your learning and sound divinity by offering you a position of greater dignity and less work. The duties, I need not tell you, are commanding in their nature; and I feel sure you would be able to perform them with great advantage to the interests of the Church, to which I think the course I am taking will be most beneficial, especially at this critical moment in its history.

I have the honour to be, dear Canon Spratte,

Yours faithfully,
Stonehenge.

The Hon. and Rev. Canon Spratte,
St. Gregory's Vicarage.

The Prime Minister offered him an obscure, insignificant deanery in the north of Wales. For an instant Canon Spratte could not understand. It seemed impossible, it seemed preposterous. He thought it must be a mistake, and carefully read the letter again. The overthrow of all his hopes came upon him at the moment of his greatest exultation, and the blow was greater than he could bear; two scalding tears rose in his eyes, and heavily, painfully, rolled down his cheeks. They fell on the letter and made two little wet smudges.

The disappointment was so great that he could not be angry. He was utterly crushed. And then, in the revulsion from his high spirits, he was overwhelmed with despair. He asked pitifully whether he had all along misjudged himself. The Prime Minister did not think him fit for important office but sought to satisfy his claims by an empty honour, such as he might give to a man who, perhaps, had deserved well, but whose powers were now decrepit. That post of dignity was but a decent grave.

Suddenly, with the vain man's utter self-abasement, Canon Spratte saw himself as he thought others might see him: mediocre, pompous, self-assertive, verbose. He heard the mocking words of the envious:

"Theodore Spratte is shelved. At all events he'll be out of harm's way at St. Olphert's, and it's just the sort of thing that'll suit him—to tyrannize over provincial old ladies."

And others would be astonished and say:

"One would have thought that pushing man would have pushed himself into something better than that!"

Again the Canon thought of all he might have done: and the pictures of the future, like scoffing devils, came once more before his mind. He could not help the tears. For a while, leaning over his desk, with his hands pressed to his burning eyes, he surrendered unresisting to his weakness. The tall spires and the sombre roofs of Barchester returned to his vivid fancy, and all that he had lost seemed twice as beautiful. The humiliation was unbearable. He hated and despised himself; he was petty and mean; and his pride, his boastfulness, his overbearing spirit, uprose against him in reproach. Who was he thus to have contemned his fellows? He had imagined himself clever, wise, and brilliant; and the world had laughed in its sleeve at his presumption. He blushed now, blushed so that he felt his face burn, at the thought that all this time people had despised him. He had lived in a fool's paradise, rejoicing in the admiration of his fellows; and he had been an object of derision. It had been self-admiration only; and the world had taken him, as did Lord Stonehenge, for the mediocre son of a clever father. Even his brother had told him repeatedly that he was pretentious and vulgar, and he thought it only the sneer of a man who could not appreciate great qualities. A thousand imps danced in his brain, with mockery and with malicious gibes: in every key from shrill to hoarse, he heard their scornful laughter.

"I won't take it," he cried, jumping up suddenly. "I'll remain where I am. I'm strong and young still; I feel as vigorous as if I were twenty. I don't want their honours."

But then he hesitated, and sank again, helplessly, into his chair. Was it not his duty to accept the promotion which was offered him? Had he a right to refuse? What was he but a servant of God, and might it not be His will that he should go to this deanery? He hated the idea, and feared the cold dulness of St. Olphert's; but yet, with something in him of English puritanism, the very fact that it was so distasteful, seemed an argument in its favour.

"Am I fit to hold a great London parish?" he asked, despairingly. "I'm growing old. Each year I shall be less active and less versatile. Ought I not to make way for younger, better men?"

He strove to drive away the thought, but could not. Some voice, the voice of conscience perhaps, told him it was his duty to accept this offer.

"O God, help me," he cried, broken at length and submissive. "I know not what to do. Guide me and teach me to do Thy will."

Presently he fell on his knees humbly and prayed. Now there was nothing in him of the confident priest or of the proud and self-assertive man; he was but an abject penitent, confessing in broken words, tremulous and halting, his utter weakness.

"O Lord, give me a holy contented frame," he cried. "Make me to desire nothing but how best to fulfil Thy holy will. Save me from worldly ambitious thoughts. I am weak and cowardly, and my sins have been very great, and I know that I am unfitted for a great position."

When he rose to his feet, with a sigh he read Stonehenge's letter for the third time. He took it in his hand and went to Lady Sophia. He felt that from her he would gain help. He was so crushed, so changed, that he needed another's guidance. For once in his life he could not make up his mind.

But when she saw him, Lady Sophia was seized with astonishment. His spirited face seemed wan and lifeless; the lines stood out, and his eyes were very tired. He appeared on a sudden to be an old man. His upright carriage was gone and he walked listlessly, with stooping shoulders.

"Theodore, what on earth's the matter?" she cried.

He handed her the letter and, in a voice still broken with emotion, said:

"Stonehenge doesn't think I'm fit to be a bishop. He's offered me a Welsh deanery."

"But you won't accept it?"

He bowed his head, looking at her with an appeal that was almost childlike.

"I'm not sure whether I have the right to refuse."

"What does he mean by saying that the duties are commanding in their nature?"

"He means nothing," answered the Canon, shrugging his shoulders scornfully. "He's merely gilding the pill with fine phrases. Oh, Sophia, I don't want to go. I don't want to bury myself in that inglorious idleness. I feel in me the power to do so much more, and St. Olphert's offers me nothing. It's a sleepy, sordid place. I might as well be buried alive. I don't want to leave London."

His voice was so pitiful that Lady Sophia was touched. She saw that he wanted her to persuade him to stay in town, and yet his conscience troubled him.

"I'm only a servant of the Church," he said. "I don't know that I have the right to refuse to go where I am sent. Perhaps he's not far wrong in thinking that it's all I'm good for. Oh, Sophia, I'm so unhappy!"

She realized how much it meant for that bold spirit thus to humble itself. He paid a heavy price for his vanity. He was like a child in her hands, needing consolation and support. She began to speak to him gently. She suggested that the offer of this deanery signified only that Lord Stonehenge, feeling he owed something to the son of the late Lord Chancellor, had been unable on account of other claims to give him the bishopric. From the observation of long years she had learnt on what points Theodore most prided himself, (in the past this knowledge had been used to give little admonishing stabs,) and now she took them one by one. She appealed skilfully to his prepossessions. With well-directed flattery, calling to his mind past triumphs, and compliments paid him by the great ones of the earth, she caused him little by little to gather courage. Presently she saw the hopeless expression of the mouth give way to a smile of pleasure, and a new confidence came into his eyes. His very back was straightened. In the new uprightness with which he held himself, she perceived that her subtle words were taking due effect. At last she reminded him of his work at St. Gregory's.

"After all, you're a figure in London," she said. "You have power and influence. For my part I have wondered that you contemplated leaving it for an obscure country town like Barchester. I shouldn't have been at all surprised if you'd refused the bishopric."

He breathed more freely, and with his quick and happy optimism began already to see things more genially.

"Besides, we Sprattes are somebody in the world," concluded Lady Sophia, with a smile, the faint irony of which he did not see. "I don't think you would show a proper spirit if you allowed yourself to be trampled on."

"Ah, Sophia, I knew that at the bottom of your heart you were as proud of your stock as I. You're quite right. I owe it to my family as well as to myself not to allow them to thrust me into obscurity. I shall refuse the deanery, Sophia; and Lord Stonehenge——"

"Can go to the devil," she added, quietly.

Canon Spratte smiled with all his old vivacity.

"Sophia, I thank you. It is not right that I should say such things, but you have entirely expressed my sentiments."

"Why don't you sit down and write the letter at once?"

Without answering, the Canon seated himself, and presently showed to Lady Sophia, for her approval, the following reply.

Dear Lord Stonehenge,

I have weighed your very considerate proposal most anxiously and have given full weight to what you urge. I fully appreciate the kind motive which offered me the opportunity of removing to a position both of leisure and of dignity. I am sure you will not think that I have lightly set aside the offer made me; but I am doubtful whether my health would stand the asperities of a Welsh climate. And I have to consider that a very great assistance to me in the performance of my present duties is derived from the complete knowledge of my work in London. I fear that I might find the distant and untried labours of St. Olphert's less congenial. And I feel that without some very strong counter-balancing reason, it is not desirable that I should leave plans which I have begun, but scarcely matured, in the Metropolis.

Believe me to be, with very grateful thanks, dear Lord Stonehenge,

Your faithful and obedient servant,
Theodore Spratte

Lady Sophia smiled when she read that last sentence in which he wisely left himself an escape, whereby he might with dignity abandon London, if a bishopric in the future were offered to him. Obviously the comfortable hope had returned that in the end his merits would receive their just reward. She gave back the letter.

"I think it will do capitally," she said. "Now, if I were you, I'd go out for a stroll."

"So I will, Sophia," he replied. "I shall never forget your encouragement. I confess I was very much cast down."

Much to her surprise he kissed her affectionately, and then said:

"As I have nowhere particular to go, I shall just walk along to Savile Row, and order two pairs of trousers."

XV

MRS. FITZHERBERT had fixed half-past eight for the hour of dinner, but Canon Spratte, anxious for a few words before any one arrived, came early. He found her ready to receive him. When he entered the drawing-room she was at the window, looking at the dusk which clothed the London street in a certain atmosphere of charming mystery.

"Well?" he said, looking at her and taking both her hands.

"I'm glad you came before the others, I wanted to have a chat with you."

"It was cruel of you to leave London so suddenly. You can't imagine how eagerly I've wished to see you."

"I'm afraid it was inevitable," she answered. "My friend is still very ill, and I only came up this evening because I didn't want to put my party off."

"I was hoping you'd come up to see me," he smiled.

"In point of fact it was only to see you," she laughed. "I would have postponed the rest of them gaily, but I think we have a good deal to say to one another."

"I feel immensely flattered," he replied.

The evening papers contained an official announcement that Dr. Gray was appointed to the bishopric of Barchester; but Canon Spratte determined that none should see his bitter disappointment. He had not yet fought down the sense of humiliation with which Lord Stonehenge's offer overwhelmed him, nor was he reconciled to remaining a London vicar. But he refused to think of his frustrated hopes. He flattered himself on his strength of character, and the world should imagine that he was in the best of spirits. He meant to keep himself well in hand, and in the decided effort to let no one see that he cared, began really to regain his self-esteem.

"I think we really ought to talk seriously," said Mrs. Fitzherbert after a pause, fixing her quiet eyes upon him. "I wonder if you meant all that you said to me the other night?"

"Of course I meant it, every word of it, with all my heart," he cried, emphatically. "Do you think I'm a boy not to know my own mind?"

"And you really look upon yourself as solemnly engaged to me?"

"I do indeed, and before many weeks are up I mean to lead

you to the altar. We'll have the bishop to marry us, and Tom shall lend us Beachcombe for our honeymoon. Or would you prefer Homburg and the Italian Lakes?"

"You know, I shouldn't be at all annoyed if you told me you were carried away the other night and said more than you intended. You're a susceptible man and there's something about a dance that rushes the least emotional off their feet. I think half the unhappy marriages are caused by the proposing of young men when they've come to the end of their small talk; and their cowardice next day which prevents them from writing to say they made a mistake."

"But it was no sudden whim on my part," he exclaimed. "The idea had been growing in my mind for months. Ah, why can't I make you believe that love may spring up in a man's heart even though his hair is strewn with silver? I tell you I'm passionately devoted to you, and I insist on marrying you."

Mrs. Fitzherbert smiled and looked at him strangely. He was very gallant and very eager. She wondered if there were ever a word of sincerity in anything he said.

"Then let us talk business," she answered.

He threw up his hands in a gesture of disdain.

"Why should we? You know I'm not mercenary; let us pretend that no tiresome matters have to be discussed. We can leave it all to our solicitors."

"But it's very important."

"Nonsense! Nothing's important except that you're the most charming woman I've ever seen in my life. I'm a lucky dog to have got hold of you. We'll never grow any older than we are now; we'll only grow younger year by year. When will you make me the happiest man in London?"

"You go so quickly," she smiled.

He put his arm round her waist and seized her hand.

"Come, give me a kiss." She positively blushed when he took it without more ado. "Upon my soul, you make me feel a perfect stripling. Shall we say in six weeks? That will bring us to the end of the season, and I can safely leave Lionel to preach to a regiment of empty pews."

"For heaven's sake sit down quietly, and let me get a word in."

"Not till you've agreed. I won't let you go till you've fixed the day."

"You shall fix the day yourself," she cried, extricating herself from his embrace.

Canon Spratte, with a laugh of triumph, threw himself into a comfortable chair. He was excited and restless. He knew he had never looked handsomer than at this moment, and he would not have changed places with a guardsman of twenty-five.

"What I wanted to tell you is that I have an income of five thousand a year," said Mrs. Fitzherbert.

"I cannot bear these gross and sordid details," he answered, with a wave of the hand. "Of course it shall be settled absolutely upon you. What more is there to be said?"

"Only that it ceases on the day I marry again."

Canon Spratte started and for a moment his face fell.

"All of it?" he asked.

"Every penny. My husband was a very generous man, but he had apparently no desire to provide for the wants of his successor. On my second marriage everything I have, the very furniture of this house, goes to a distant cousin of his."

She watched the Canon for the effect of this blow, and she could not deny that he took it admirably.

"I'm very glad," he said. "I much prefer to provide for your wants myself. I shouldn't like to think you were living on another man's income."

"Do you realize that I shall be so penniless, you will even have to provide the clothes for my back and my very fare when I take the tube?"

"It will only make you more precious to me."

The doors were swung open and the butler announced the first arrivals, Mrs. Fitzherbert stepped forward to greet them. Ten minutes later the whole party was seated round the dinner-table.

Canon Spratte was filled with consternation. It was true that he had not sought to marry Mrs. Fitzherbert for her money, but on the other hand the idea would never have come to him except that he knew she had a handsome income. It had never entered his head that she might hold it on such preposterous terms, and the blow was terrible. The Lord Chancellor had been able to leave him nothing. The bulk of his fortune went of necessity to his successor in the title and the rest to Lady Sophia, who announced her determination to lead a single life. St. Gregory's was worth a certain amount and the canonry something more, but this from the depreciation of land was slowly diminishing. He had always spent every penny he earned. His children had three hundred a year each, but they were to be married and would naturally take the money with them. Lionel was paid nothing for acting as his father's curate, but he might soon get a living and another expense would ensue. Lady Sophia had contributed a good deal to the household cost of the vicarage, but would of course make her home elsewhere when the Canon brought home a legitimate mistress. He did not see how on earth he could make both ends meet. Mrs. Fitzherbert, far from making up richly for all he lost, would be a source of vast expenditure. It would be necessary to give up the carriage and the horses of which he was so proud. Every cab that his wife took would be a shilling out of his pocket. A little while before Canon Spratte had ventured on a small flutter in the Stock Exchange, and the shares were not rising with the rapidity his broker had promised. This had seemed a bagatelle, but now grew suddenly into a matter of importance. The Canon's heart sank. He looked at Mrs. Fitzherbert; and the gown which he had admired on his entrance appeared very expensive. She had none of the airs of an economical woman, and it would be needful to economize. He loathed the idea of counting each sovereign as he spent it. He liked the large gesture of generosity, and had the reputation of a man who spent his money well. Now he must be niggardly.

But above all he felt sold. It had been his consolation in the loss of the bishopric that the widow's large means, added to his own, would enable him to cut a figure in London. He proposed to entertain lavishly. He wanted to make St. Gregory's Vicarage a centre of fashion and intelligence, so that his name should go down to posterity like Sydney Smith's as the most brilliant parson of his day. Instead he was saddled with a penniless wife.

But not one of these distressing emotions was visible on the Canon's face during dinner. He had never needed his self-control more. Perhaps he showed his strength no less admirably than he could have done if, according to his ardent wish, he had been in happier days a great minister of state. The party consisted of eight, which he thought precisely the right number. It was neither so large that the conversation ceased to be general nor so small as to give a good talker an insufficient audience. Mrs. Fitzherbert noticed with admiration that he had never seemed in better spirits, and took a vow that whatever happened she would certainly remain friendly with him. He was invaluable at a dinner-party. It was only from an occasional look of weariness, quickly driven away, from a metallic, unusual ring in his laughter, that she suspected how great was his effort. He made himself the centre of the table, and he was so vivacious that none wished to question his supremacy. His stories had never been better, and he told them with a gusto that added vastly to their humour. He was never at a loss for a repartee; his sallies and quaint turns kept the party so well entertained that Mrs. Fitzherbert was radiant. She had never given a more successful dinner, and had the satisfaction of knowing that her guests thoroughly enjoyed themselves. When they thanked her on leaving, it was with a sincerity which she knew was unusual on similar occasions. She felt grateful to Canon Spratte.

"And now that every one has gone you must sit down and smoke a cigarette, and we'll have a quiet chat."

"That's just what I should like. I've got something to say to you."

"Have you? That's very odd, because I have too."

He seated himself, and she noticed that for the first time in their acquaintance, he was embarrassed. She looked at him with smiling eyes, but to him they seemed disconcertingly ironic.

"I think we should go back to the conversation we had before dinner," he said. "Would you think it very odd if I made a suggestion?"

He waited for a reply, but she gave none, and he was forced to proceed. There was no doubt about it, he was growing exceedingly nervous.

"Well, I suggested then that we should be married in six weeks. I'm afraid it sounds very ungallant if I propose now that we should wait a little."

"How long?" she asked quietly.

"Oh, I don't know—perhaps a year, two at the utmost. You see, I'm not exactly hard up, but——" He hesitated again, for once in his life at a loss for words. "The fact is I don't see how we can possibly marry till I get a bishopric. I'm practically certain to get one soon—there's no one with half the claims I have, and I think I can boast of a certain amount of influence."

"Two years is a long time at our age," she smiled. "Especially for a woman. You know, even now, you're ever so much younger in spirit than I am; I'm afraid that each day will increase the difference between us."

He paused for the very shortest space of time.

"Of course, if you'd rather marry at once, I shall be only too charmed. It will make me the happiest of men. It was only on your account that I hesitated. I'm afraid that you'll have to do without a good many of the luxuries that you're used to."

"It's very thoughtful of you," she murmured.

"I'm afraid we shan't be able to have a carriage."

"You know, I adore riding on 'buses," she answered, with twinkling eyes. "One sits on the front seat and talks to the driver."

"And then I'm afraid there'll be no more little trips to Homburg in the summer or to the Riviera in the winter."

"When all's said and done is there any place in the world so comfortable as London?"

"It's charming to think that you're so easily satisfied."

She watched him thoughtfully, while he sought to conceal behind a gallant smile a considerable feeling of dismay.

"Are you sure you wouldn't rather break off altogether our short engagement?" she asked, suddenly.

"Nothing would induce me," he cried, with the utmost emphasis. "Do you imagine that anything you have said makes you less precious to me? You cannot think so badly of me as to suppose that I no longer wish to marry you, because you are not rich."

"You're an ambitious man, and an opulent wife might have been of great use to you: a poor one can only be a drawback."

"You pain me very much," he answered. "I confess I think it would be wise to delay our union, but it would break my heart to put aside all thought of it."

"Oh, I don't think your heart is such a fragile organ as that. Let us be frank with one another. I venture to flatter myself that you did not want to marry me because of my money, but it's obvious that a well-regulated passion is not diminished because an attractive widow has five thousand a year. It's very comprehensible that you shouldn't wish to marry a pauper."

"I flatter myself on the other hand that I'm by way of being a gentleman."

"Shall we say no more about it? Shall we forget that you murmured various things the other night which you didn't quite mean?"

Mrs. Fitzherbert knew that she was very cruel. It was plain that he wished with all his might to accept his release. He suffered the torture of Tantalus, for escape lay within his easy reach, and he had not the effrontery to take it. He was a man who lived for the noble gesture, and he could not bring himself to make one that was uncommonly prosaic.

"I assure you no one shall know anything about it," she added. "I promise you I will be as silent as the grave."

He looked at her with an indecision that was almost pitiful.

"If I accepted your suggestion you'd despise me all your life," he said.

There was something in his tone that made Mrs. Fitzherbert think she had gone far enough. He was really suffering this time, and she could not bear to see it. She went up to him quickly, and smiling, put her hands on his shoulders.

"My dear man, do you suppose for a moment that I had any intention of marrying you? Nothing would have induced me to do it."

"What do you mean?" he cried.

"I've reached an age when I can't imagine that it would be worth while sacrificing five thousand a year for any man. Besides, you're charming as a friend, but as a husband you'd be quite insufferable. I wouldn't marry you if I were starving and you had all the wealth of Golconda."

"D'you mean to say you've been playing with me all the time?"

"I'm afraid that is precisely what it comes to."

He drew away from her, and his face took that rather peevish expression of a spoilt child which it sometimes had.

"I think it's very cruel of you," he said.

"Let us forget all about it. You're perfectly free and there's no need whatever for you to marry me. Let us be friends. And don't flirt any more with widow-ladies; they're dreadfully dangerous."

"I daresay it's a very good joke to you, but you've exposed me to the most awful humiliation. You ask me to be friends, but I shall never be able to look you in the face again."

Mrs. Fitzherbert ceased to smile and her eyes became quite grave.

"Shall I tell you a secret that I've never divulged to any living soul?" she said. "Perhaps you'll understand why I couldn't resist the chance you gave me. I daresay you've forgotten that five-and-twenty years ago we used to see a great deal of one another. Perhaps you never knew that I was so desperately in love with you then that I would have married you if you hadn't a penny in the world, and I would have been glad to scrub the floors you walked on."

The Canon started and was about to speak. But with a little laugh she stopped him.

"Oh, please don't make any observation yet. Even now it makes me feel rather silly to speak about it. I daresay you flirted with a good many other girls as much as you did with me, but I was foolish enough to think you cared for me. And I thought you meant to ask me to marry you. Then you met Dorothy Frampstone, and you married her instead. Well, it's very possible that she was much nicer than I, but you mustn't be surprised if my vanity leads me to think there were much more solid reasons. I have an idea you transferred your affections to her chiefly because she had six hundred a year while I was penniless, and she was the daughter of a peer of the realm while I was nobody in particular."

"You do me an injustice," he murmured.

"Anyhow it doesn't matter, it's all very long ago. The important thing is that I did love you then really, so if I've made you feel a little ridiculous now, it's only tit for tat."

She held out her hand, smiling, and he warmly grasped it.

"You're a wonderful woman, and I was a fool five-and-twenty years ago. The fates have been against me all along."

"And now good-night," she laughed. "It's growing late, and it's really very compromising for a lone, lorn widow to remain so long en tête-à-tête with a fascinating person like yourself."

"Good-night, then."

He bent down, and with the utmost grace kissed her hand. When he left her Mrs. Fitzherbert quietly smiled.

"I thank my stars I am a lone, lorn woman, and unless I become a perfect lunatic I'll take care to remain one."

XVI

THE Canon passed an unquiet night; and next morning, feeling in need of fresh air, took a stroll in the Park. The day was very fine, and there was a charming freshness in the air which soon brought back his serenity. He sauntered up the Row looking at the people who were out already to enjoy the earliness of the day after a late night at some gay party. He stopped now and then to observe the flowers, in which he took the horticulturist's delight: Canon Spratte had an amiable weakness for putting Latin names to the daintiest blossoms of the way-side. He nodded to one or two friends and passed the time of day with a famous politician. The scene had an air of luxury and of fashionable indifference to the cares of life which filled him with satisfaction.

Presently he saw Gwendolen Durant ride towards him.

She looked so well on horseback that he wondered more than ever why Lionel could not make up his mind to marry. She stopped and spoke to him. They exchanged the simple banter which serves for wit among the easily pleased, and the Canon expressed his admiration of her seat. She nodded a farewell and put her heel to the horse's side. But at that moment a motor-car rushed by at a terrific speed and gave a series of loud explosions. Gwendolen's horse turned round with a sudden leap that almost unseated her, and was on the point of bolting, when the Canon jumped forward and seized the bridle. It was not a very dangerous action, but it required some presence of mind, and he performed it with a breadth of gesture that made it look almost heroic.

"Thanks, so much," said Gwendolen, a little out of breath and startled. "If you hadn't been there he'd have bolted. He's got a mouth like iron and he simply pulls my arms out."

"Are you quite sure you're safe now?" asked Canon Spratte, anxiously.

The horse was still nervous and refused to stand still.

"He'll probably bolt with me, but I must risk it," she laughed, trying to show no concern.

"Let me tighten the curb a little, and then you'll be as safe as a house." With deft fingers he undid the chain and altered it. "You know, you really ought not to ride alone."

"A groom bores me, and there's no one else to come."

"I shall ride with you to-morrow," he answered. "I don't think you should be left to your own devices. Now I think you're in no danger."

She thanked him effusively and trotted quickly off. The Canon resumed his promenade somewhat pleased with the action: he was grateful for the smallest incident that served to restore his diminished self-esteem. He was turning round to go home when he felt a hand on his shoulder. It was Sir John Durant.

"I've just seen Gwendolen. She tells me you saved her from a nasty accident."

"Oh, it was nothing. I happened to be near."

"I don't know how to thank you."

"If you'll allow me to say it, I think it's somewhat incautious to let her ride alone. I've offered to accompany her to-morrow."

"Oh, that's very good of you," said the brewer. "I'm afraid you'll find it a great bore."

"Not at all; I assure you it will be a great pleasure. My doctor has advised me to take horse-exercise, and I shall be only too glad to have some one to ride with." The Canon put his arm through the brewer's in his most friendly fashion. "And how are you, my dear fellow? I trust that your affairs are flourishing."

"Well, in point of fact they're not," cried the other, suddenly growing serious. "That confounded Government wants to give the local justices power to close a certain proportion of public-houses in their districts."

"Ah, yes, I saw something about that in the papers, but I understood it would have no influence on the consumption of liquor. Stonehenge's idea is that the remaining houses will profit."

"Don't you believe it," cried Sir John, with much vigour. "Nine times out of ten a man doesn't drink a glass of beer because he's thirsty, but because there's a public-house at his elbow. Each one they shut up will take a good round sum out of our pockets."

"The Government seems very strong on the point. I suppose they've been got hold of by the faddists."

Sir John stopped still and significantly tapped Canon Spratte on the chest. His utterance was full of weight.

"Mark my words. The Government doesn't know how strong we are. If they try to interfere with the liquor interest it'll be a bad day for the Conservative party. I'll fight them tooth and nail, and I shall carry the whole trade with me. I'm not a boasting fool, but I tell you this: the Government's in a damned wobbly state, and if they put my back up I don't answer for the consequences."

Canon Spratte looked at his red-faced friend with the utmost attention. He knew that Sir John Durant was a rich man, but had not realized till this moment that he was a powerful man as well.

Events might take such a turn that any one who had the brewer's ear would command vast influence. He looked at his watch. It was time for him to keep an appointment, and he wanted to think quietly over the consequences of this discovery.

"Why don't you come and lunch with me at the club one day?" he asked. "I'm afraid I mayn't take you to the Athenæum, but they give you capital wine at the Carlton."

Sir John accepted with pleasure, and so they parted. He was very thoughtful during the remainder of that morning, but at luncheon announced to his family that he proposed to ride every morning after breakfast. His doctor had recommended exercise, and he knew of no other which combined in such just proportions entertainment with utility.

"And what about this marriage of yours, Theodore?" asked Lady Sophia. "You forget that we are all on tenterhooks."

He stared at her for a moment with a very natural show of amazement, and burst into a shout of laughter.

"It was only a little joke of mine, Sophia. You don't imagine it's likely that I should marry at my age."

"As you say, we Sprattes have a remarkable sense of humour," she replied, dryly.

"I can't help poking fun at you sometimes, my dear. But, as you rightly observed, no one would be such a fool as to marry an old fossil like your humble servant."

But her remarks had brought back to his mind an incident which he would willingly have forgotten. He was still very sore, and the more he thought of it the more foolish he felt himself. It was in no amiable mood, therefore, that he waited for Bertram Railing, who was expected to call that afternoon. Nor was the Canon much pleased with his daughter, and he had mentioned two or three times his annoyance that her wilful disobedience had placed him in an awkward position. Railing was not an easy person to deal with. His plainness and outspoken candour rendered possible a very undignified altercation.

But when the young man arrived nothing was visible on the Canon's face save complete friendliness. They shook hands.

"Ah, how good of you to come, dear Railing. So glad to see you."

"Winnie told me she'd be at home this afternoon."

"Of course I didn't flatter myself that you'd come to see me," laughed the Canon. "But in point of fact I've been wanting to have a little talk with you. It's a very serious step that you young folks are taking."

"Then we're wise to take it with a light heart," cried Railing, gaily.

"Ha, ha, capital! Now I should have thought you were both very young to be married."

"I am twenty-eight, sir, and Winnie is twenty-one."

"You neither of you look it," murmured the Canon, with an amiable bow.

"Possibly!"

Canon Spratte pulled out the splendid cigarette-case in gold, with initials of diamonds, which a fond admirer had presented to him. He offered it to Railing.

"No, thank you. I never smoke."

"I see you have no vices." The Canon became so bland that it was overwhelming. "Now, my dear fellow, let us discuss this matter in the most cordial way. I need not tell you that I have the very highest esteem for you personally, and the sincerest admiration for your talents. But we live in an age when talent is not always rewarded according to its merits, and I am curious to know upon what you propose to live."

"My income is about a hundred and fifty a year and Winnie has three hundred from her mother."

"You are very well informed," smiled the Canon, good-naturedly.

"Winnie told me," said Bertram, flushing.

"Obviously! I didn't suppose for a moment that you had examined the will at Somerset House. And do you imagine that Winnie will be content to live on four hundred and fifty pounds a year?"

"It's three times as much as my mother ever had."

"Possibly, but your mother—a most excellent person, Mr. Railing—has moved in rather a different stratum of society from my daughter."

"Do you think your daughter cares two straws for the gewgaws and the tawdry trappings of Society?" asked Bertram, scornfully.

The Canon shrugged his shoulders.

"I think my daughter is human, Mr. Railing; and although it may surprise you, I will confess that I think a carriage and pair absolutely essential to her happiness."

"I know Winnie, and I love her. You think she's a doll and a fool. She was. But I have made her into a woman of flesh and blood. She's a real woman now and she loathes all the shams and the shallowness of Society."

"She told you that, did she?" answered the Canon. "Upon my word, we Sprattes have a keen sense of humour."

Bertram sprang to his feet and crossed over to the Canon.

"You think she cares for carriages and fine clothes. Her life was a mockery. She didn't know what life was. She had no aspirations, no ideals. Of course she wasted herself on the frivolities of a foolish world. Thank God, she knows now how narrow this little circle is of idle, selfish people. She wants to work, she wants to labour with her fellow-men, shoulder to shoulder, fighting the good fight."

"And do you think, my dear young man, that it would ever have occurred to Winnie that the world was hollow and foolish, if you had a wart on the tip of your nose, or a squint in your eye? Upon my soul, you're very unsophisticated."

"You believe that all people are bad."

"On the contrary, I'm so charitable as to think them merely foolish," said Canon Spratte, with an acid smile of amusement.

"Have you only sneers for the new life that fills your daughter's eyes? She's a different creature now. Oh, I believe in her, thank God, as she believes in me! She's ready to take the journey with me only by her side. Ah, I know she loves me. You think I'm only a fortune-hunter; we don't want your money, we shouldn't know what to do with it."

"And you're quite content that for you she should sacrifice everything?"

"She flings away painted husks, dross, tinsel," cried Bertram, vehemently. "She gains the whole world."

"Which means you and a villa in Peckham Rye. Upon my soul, you're very modest."

Bertram looked at him steadily, thrusting forward his head with a searching air. He turned over in his mind all that the other had said.

"What are you driving at?" he asked, at length. "Why don't you say it out like a man, instead of beating about the bush?"

"My dear Mr. Railing, I must beg you to observe the conventions of polite society. It is clearly my duty to inquire into the circumstances of any young man who proposes to marry my daughter."

Bertram gave a little hoarse laugh.

"I distrusted you when you first agreed to our engagement. I knew you despised me. I knew that all your flattery was humbug. Say it straight out like a man."

Canon Spratte shrugged his shoulders, and spoke slowly and gravely.

"Mr. Railing, I solemnly ask you to give up my daughter. After mature reflection I have come to the conclusion that the marriage is impossible, and I will never give my consent to it."

"We will do without it; we're free, both of us, and we don't care a button for you. Winnie has promised to marry me, and, by God, she shall."

"Do you absolutely disregard my express wishes?"

"The matter concerns us alone, and no one else in the whole world."

Canon Spratte thoughtfully examined his finger-nails.

On a sudden he had an inspiration. He had learned a fact from Mrs. Railing, which he thought at the time might prove useful, and here was the opportunity.

"Well, Mr. Railing, it's very painful to me to have to talk to you in this manner. It is true that some time ago I gave a provisional sanction to your engagement with Winnie, and I can perfectly understand that it should seem strange if I now resolutely forbid it. I have no doubt this is a great disappointment to you, and for that reason I excuse your heated language, which has been certainly wanting in courtesy. I am sure that when you are calmer you will regret some of the expressions you have seen fit to use. But I will tell you at once that I bear you on this account absolutely no ill-will."

"I'm much obliged to you, but I'm not aware that I've used any expression which I'm in the least likely to regret," said Bertram, sharply.

"Then, if I may say so, as a man much older than yourself, and as a clergyman, you show both your want of Christian charity and your ignorance of social amenities.... I beg you not to interrupt me," he added, when he saw that Railing was about to make a rejoinder. "You will understand that I am not the man to wrangle like a fishwife."

"Will you tell me shortly what new objection you have to me, Canon Spratte?"

"That is what I am about to do. It has come to my knowledge that your eldest sister is unfortunately in a lunatic asylum. I need not tell you that I regret this misfortune, but my views on the subject are very decided. With insanity among your relations, I feel that an alliance between your family and mine is out of the question."

"That's absurd!" cried Railing. "Florrie had an accident when she was a child. She fell downstairs, and since then she's been——"

"Not quite right in her head, as your mother expressed it, Mr. Railing. I should like you to observe, however, that every child falls downstairs, and the entire human race is not so imbecile as to need the restraint of a lunatic asylum."

Bertram's eyes were fixed steadily on Canon Spratte. He tried to discover what lay at the back of the man's mind, but could not. He saw only that behind that calm face, amid this resonance of polished phrase, something was being hidden from him.

"I don't believe a word you say. I'm not a child. I assure you it's no good trying to hoodwink me. Tell me the simple truth."

The Canon flushed at this appeal and was nearly put out of countenance. He wondered if he should fly into a passion and order Railing out of the house. But it was doubtful whether the Socialist would go. He was a little disconcerted, too, by the steadfastness with which Bertram had resisted him, and the scorn wherewith he brushed aside his specious reasons. Canon Spratte was hot with anger. The taunts to which he had calmly listened, rankled in his heart, and he would have been pleased to show that none could thus treat him with impunity. But he seldom lost his temper unadvisedly, and he realized now that calmness gave him a decided advantage over the angry and excited suitor.

"Are you quite sure that Winnie cares for you?" he asked, mildly.

"As sure as I am of my own name and of my own life."

There was a pause. The Canon for a minute walked up and down the room; and then, holding himself very erect, stood still in front of Bertram. His voice was full of authority.

"Well, it is my painful duty to inform you that you are mistaken. Winnie recognizes that she misjudged the strength of her affection."

"I don't believe it," said Railing, full of scorn.

"My patience must be inexhaustible. I am much tempted to kick you downstairs, Mr. Railing."

"You forget that I'm a working-man and horny-handed, so it's safer not to try."

"It evidently hasn't occurred to you that the manners of Peckham Rye are not altogether suitable to South Kensington," smiled the Canon, blandly.

"Well?"

"Winnie has requested me to tell you that she finds she does not care for you enough to marry you. She regrets the inconvenience and unhappiness that she has caused, and desires you to release her."

Bertram grew white and he gathered himself together as a wild beast might, driven to bay.

"It's a lie!" he cried, furiously. "It's a lie!"

The Canon replied with the utmost calm.

"You will have the goodness to remember that I am a minister of the Church and a son of the late Lord Chancellor of England."

"If it's true, you've forced her to give me up. I know she loves me."

"You may think what you choose, Mr. Railing. The fact remains that she wishes to break off her engagement with you. As a man of honour there is obviously but one course open to you."

"You tell me I'm a man of honour and you treat me like a lackey. Do you think you can dismiss me like a servant? Don't you know that my whole life's happiness is at stake? She can't send me away like that. It's not true, it's not true."

"On my honour as a gentleman, I have told you the exact truth," replied Canon Spratte, gravely. Bertram seized the Canon's arm.

"Let her tell me herself. I must see her. Where is she?"

"She's gone out."

"But she knew I was coming here to-day. She expected me."

"Doesn't that show you that what I have said is the simple truth? I wished to spare you both a painful scene."

Bertram hesitated. He could not tell whether Winnie was really out, but it seemed impossible to verify the statement. For a moment he looked straight into the Canon's eyes, then without a word turned on his heel. Canon Spratte gave a sigh of relief.

"What an escape!" he muttered. "Good Lord, what an escape!"

XVII

NEXT morning, when Winnie came down to breakfast, she found a letter from Bertram. She opened it with trembling hands. It began abruptly and consisted only of two lines.

I shall wait for you to-day in Kensington Gardens at ten o'clock. I beg you to come.

In the early days of their engagement, when Canon Spratte refused to hear Railing's name mentioned, they had been used to walk together every morning. They met always at a particular spot. There were shady alleys, the scene of many pleasant conversations, which Winnie could not help remembering with delight. She dreaded the meeting he asked for, but felt that it was not in her to refuse. She had thought all night over the brief account her father had given of his interview with Bertram, and wished with all her heart now to explain personally why she had taken this step. She could not bear that he should think too hardly of her. The wounds she made seemed inevitable, but perhaps she could do something to make him see how impossible it was for her to act otherwise.

Without saying a word to her father, Winnie went out immediately after breakfast, and when she arrived at the appointed place, found Bertram already there. He greeted her without a smile. He was very pale and she felt her own face burn with shame under his sad, questioning eyes. For a few minutes they talked of indifferent things, as though they could not bring themselves to attack the subject that filled their hearts. They sat down and for a while were silent. At last he turned round and looked at her gravely.

"It's true, then?" he said.

"I'm very sorry," she murmured, turning her face away.

"When your father spoke to me I couldn't bring myself to believe it. The whole thing seemed too horrible. Even now, I can't convince myself that you really want me to give you up. I've not had it from your own lips yet."

"I want you to release me, Bertram. I can't marry you."

"But why, why? The other day you said you loved me better than any one in the whole world. What have they done to turn you against me? Oh, I thought better of you than that, Winnie; I trusted you."

"I was mistaken when I thought I loved you," she whispered.

"They're forcing you to give me up?"

"No," she answered, shaking her head. "No one has done anything to influence me."

"And yet, suddenly, with nothing to explain it, you send your father to say you've made a mistake; and don't want to marry me. Oh, it's shameful, it's too cruel."

"Oh, Bertram, don't speak like that," she cried, looking at him at last.

The unhappiness of his voice was very hard to bear and she could hardly restrain a sob. He looked at her with puzzled eyes. He was so wretched that his brain was all confused.

"You loved me the other day," he cried. "Oh, don't be so cold. Tell me what there is to tell, Winnie. I love you so passionately. I can't live without you."

"Forgive me. I'm awfully sorry for all the pain I've caused you."

"Are you afraid because I'm poor and of mean birth? But you knew that before. Oh, I don't understand; it seems impossible. I never dreamed you'd do this. I trusted you ten times more than I trusted myself."

"I'm not fit to be your wife," she sobbed.

"How can you sacrifice all that we planned so joyfully, the life of labour shoulder to shoulder and the fine struggle for our fellows?"

"I should hate it," she answered, hoarsely.

He stared at her with surprise. He caught the immense vehemence of her expression and the little shiver of disgust that crossed her shoulders. They were silent again.

"Oh, Bertram, try to understand," said Winnie, at last. "I don't want you to be unhappy, I want you to see that we've made a dreadful mistake. I thank God that we've discovered it before it was too late. I'm not made for the life you want me to lead. I should be utterly out of it. And all those meetings, and the agitations for things I don't care two straws about! Oh, I loathe the very thought of it."

He looked before him as though the very foundations of the world were sinking. Winnie put her hand on his arm gently.

"Don't trouble about me, Bertram. I'm not worth it. You thought me different from what I am. You've never known me; you put another soul into my body, and you loved that. If you really knew me, you'd only despise me. You thought I could do heroic things, but I can't. When I was enthusiastic about labour and temperance and all the rest, it was merely pose. I wanted you to think me clever and original. I was flattered because you spoke to me as if you thought my opinion worth having. But honestly I don't like poor people; I hate grime and dirt; I can't look upon them as my fellows; I don't want to have anything to do with them. I dare say poverty and crime are very dreadful, and the misery of the slums is heart-rending, but I don't want to see it. I want to shut my eyes and forget all about it. Can't you see how awful it would be if we married? I should only hamper you, and we'd both be utterly wretched."

"Your father said a carriage and pair was essential to your happiness. I told him I would stake my life on you. I told him that you despised the sham and the shallowness of Society."

"I suppose papa knows me," said Winnie.

"Oh, dearest, it can't be true," he cried, taking her hand. "You can't mind whether you go on foot or in a gaudy carriage. Life is so full and there's so much work to do. What can it matter so long as we do our duty?"

"I know I'm a cad, but I must have decent things, and servants, and nice clothes. It's vulgar and hateful and petty, but I can't help it. I want to live as all my friends live. I haven't the courage to give up all that makes life beautiful. It's not just one act of heroism that it needs; it's strength to be heroic day after day in a sort of dull, sordid fashion. And there can never be any escape from it; one has to make up one's mind that it will last for ever. I see myself living in a shabby house in a horrid pokey street, with two dirty little maids, and I could almost scream. Oh, I couldn't, Bertram."

"I thought you cared for me."

She did not answer.

"It's different for you," she pleaded. "You've been brought up without all these things, and you don't miss them. I daresay it's utterly snobbish, but I can't help it. I've been used to luxuries all my life; it's just as impossible for me to go without them as it would be for you to go without a coat in winter. You think it's very easy for me to do housework and to mend linen as your mother does, but d'you think it's any easier than it would be for you who've worked with your brains, to mend roads from morning till night? I know girls who've done that sort of thing. I've seen the shifts with which they keep up appearances and the awful struggle to make both ends meet. I've seen their faces pinched with anxiety, and I've seen the wrench it causes when they must spend a shilling. I couldn't stand it, Bertram. You're quite right; I am afraid."

"But I love you, Winnie," he said. "You're the whole world to me. Tell me what you want me to do and I'll try to do it. I can't lose you."

"What can you do? How can you change yourself? Don't you see that it's impossible, and that we're utterly unsuited to one another? Really we've not got a single thought or aim or idea in common. You can't want to make me so unhappy as to wish to marry me."

"Then it's good-bye?" he asked.

Winnie looked up. To her surprise she saw her father ride past with Gwendolen Durant. Instinctively she drew back, seeking to hide herself; but they were too deeply engrossed in conversation to notice her.

Railing's eyes met hers sadly.

"I don't know how I shall live without you," he said.

"You must try and forgive me for all the wretchedness I've caused you. And soon I hope that you'll forget all about me."

"Is there no chance that you'll ever change your mind?" he asked, brokenly.

She hesitated, for there was something on her heart which she felt strangely impelled to confess. It seemed that she owed it to him.

"I think I ought to tell you that Lord Wroxham has asked me to marry him."

"And are you going to?" he gasped.

"I've known him ever since I was a child, and I'm very fond of him. I'm frightened. I wanted you to know from my own lips rather than from a newspaper. You probably can't despise me more than you do already."

"What do you mean by saying you're frightened? Are you frightened of me?"

"Yes."

"Then it is good-bye indeed," he answered, after a long silence.

He stood up and without another word left her. Winnie began to cry silently. In that pleasure garden, fit scene for the careless trifling of fair ladies in hoops and of gentlemen in periwigs, every one else seemed happy and unconcerned. Children in their bright dresses played with merry shouts and their nurses idly gossiped. A tremor passed through Winnie's body as she struggled in vain to restrain her sobbing.

In the afternoon Winnie told her father that she had seen Bertram. She felt still as though her heart were breaking.

"Oh, father, I feel so ashamed," she moaned.

Canon Spratte pursed his lips and nodded once or twice gravely. He did not approve of this stolen interview, but presumed it would be the last. He addressed her in grave, sonorous tones.

"You do well to feel ashamed, my child. I hope this will be a warning and a lesson to you. You see what comes of disobeying your father, and setting yourself obstinately and irreligiously against his better judgment. In future I trust you will be more dutiful. Believe me, it is always best to honour your parents; and if you don't you're sure to be punished for it."

"Oughtn't I to tell Harry?" she asked.

"Tell him what?" cried the Canon, perfectly aghast.

"I think he ought to know that I was engaged to Bertram."

"Certainly not," he answered, with the utmost decision. "I entirely forbid you to do anything of the sort, and I hope you've been sufficiently punished for your wilful disobedience to obey me now. Wroxham is very susceptible, and it's your duty to give him no anxiety. And whatever you do, don't begin your married life by confessing everything to your husband. It will only bore him to death. Besides, one never can tell the whole truth, and it leads inevitably to deception and subterfuge."

"But suppose he finds out?"

Canon Spratte gave a sigh of genuine relief, for after all the fear of discovery is the easiest form of conscience to deal with.

"Is that all you're frightened of, my darling?" he said. "Leave it to me. I'll tell him all that's necessary."

And the next time he found himself alone with Wroxham, he took the opportunity to set the matter right.

"By the way, Harry, Winnie wants me to tell you something that's rather worrying her. You know what girls are. They often have a sensitiveness of conscience which is very charming but at the same time rather ridiculous. I don't suppose you ever heard of a young man called Railing?' "

"You mean the Socialist? Winnie gave me his book to read."

"I may say I was among the first to discover its striking merit. I thought it my duty to encourage him, and I asked him to come and see us. His father, it appears, was a coal-heaver, and I thought him a very remarkable fellow. But he repaid my kindness by falling in love with Winnie and asking her to marry him."

"Why didn't you kick him down-stairs?" laughed Wroxham, lightly.

"Upon my word, I had half a mind to. I will never befriend the lower orders again; they always take liberties with you."

At this juncture Winnie came into the room. Canon Spratte told her that he had informed Wroxham of the unfortunate incident. She gave her devoted lover an appealing glance; and the thought that she was so fearful to offend him, increased a thousandfold his passionate tenderness.

"You're not angry with me, dear?"

"Because a madman wants to marry you? Why, I want to do that myself."

"Capital! Capital!" laughed the Canon. "But seriously I don't think he's quite right in his head. His sister is in a lunatic asylum, you know. I hope you won't receive any nonsensical letter from him."

Wroxham was all eyes for Winnie, and scarcely listened to the trivial topic.

"If I do, it shall go straight into the waste-paper basket," he answered, lightly.

"Quite right," said the Canon. "Quite right!"

He tactfully left the lovers to themselves.

XVIII

SOME days later Lord Spratte found himself dressed half-an-hour too early for the dinner-party to which he was going. He made up his mind to walk down Piccadilly. The evening was delightful, and he looked with amiable eyes upon the populous street. The closing day flooded the scene with gold that seemed flung from divine hands with a gesture large and free. The crowd, sweeping along the pavements, the gay 'buses and the carriages, were bathed in opulent splendour. They looked like magic things, all light and movement, seen by a painter who could work miracles. Lord Spratte congratulated himself that his fellow-men were all very well-to-do and had obviously no concern with sordid details. He braced himself to enjoy the charming world in general, and the festivity before him in particular.

"I'm feelin' younger every day," he murmured. "By Jupiter, if Theodore don't mind his p's and q's I'll marry and do him out of the title yet."

So may the fancy of middle age in June turn lightly to amorous undertakings.

Suddenly he recognized Bertram Railing, who was walking quickly towards him. They met, and the Socialist, seeing him for the first time, flushed; then he fixed his eyes firmly on Lord Spratte and with much deliberation cut him. The elder man smiled and shrugged his shoulders. He wanted to speak with Bertram, and was entirely indifferent to his obvious disinclination. He turned round and with some trouble caught him up.

"Why the dickens do you walk at that rate?" he panted, somewhat out of breath.

He took Bertram's arm familiarly. But the young man stopped and abruptly released himself.

"What do you want?"

"Merely to have a little chat. Let us stroll in the Park for five minutes."

"I'm sorry, that's impossible. I have an urgent engagement."

"Nonsense!"

Lord Spratte again seized the unwilling arm, and in the most determined way made for the Park gates.

"I want to talk to you about your engagement with Winnie. I'm afraid you've been very unhappy."

Bertram did not answer, but with firm-set jaws looked straight in front of him.

"You know, if I were you I would try not to take it too much to heart," he went on. "In a little while you'll understand that both you and Winnie would have been quite unnecessarily wretched."

He paused and looked at Bertram sharply.

"Will you promise not to turn round and bolt if I stop to light a cigarette?"

"Yes," said Bertram, smiling in spite of himself.

"You think she's a very remarkable young woman, but she's quite an average girl. Perhaps she's a little prettier than most. I know very few young women of her particular station who wouldn't have acted as she has."

"Then Heaven help her particular station," cried Bertram.

"I don't suppose it's struck you that it's a very awkward one," replied Lord Spratte, mildly. "A great family might have lived down a match of this sort, (I don't want to hurt your feelings,) but we're such very small fry. You think us snobs, and so we are. You can't expect anythin' else from people who've only just emerged from the middle-classes. You know, I have an impression that your grandfather and mine were great pals. I'm sure they used to hobnob and drink brandy and water together in seedy public-houses. Do you remember the Egyptian usurper who made a wine-cup into the image of a god, for the edification of his former boon-fellows? Well, we're somethin' like that astute monarch; we have to use all sorts of stratagems to persuade the world of our gentility. If this affair between you and Winnie had come to anything, do you know what she would have done? She would have tried all her life to live up to Mayfair, and it would have meant either that you were dragged away from your proper work, or that she would have been eternally dissatisfied. My dear boy, she would have reproached you every day for marrying her."

He stopped, feeling that the words were not coming as he wished. He wanted to be kind, and there were a few useful things he thought Bertram ought to know. But he could not properly order what was in his mind. Bertram felt the intention and presently answered less bitterly:

"Why do you take the trouble to say all this?"

"I wish I had my brother Theodore's eloquence. He'd say what I want to in the most beautiful language. He's not a bad chap, although you probably don't set much store on him. He's so fortunate as to feel himself a person of importance; I don't. I always wish I'd been the son of nobody in particular. It bores me to death to go about under the shadow of my father's name. I can't think why it is, but I go through life feeling as if I were perpetually wearin' fancy-dress. I haven't read your book. I believe it's very instructive, and at my time of life I avoid instruction. But when Winnie said she was going to marry you, I went one day to hear you speak at a meetin' in Holborn. I was never so surprised in my life."

"Why?"

"I discovered that you were sincere. By Jupiter, how you would have bored Winnie if things had gone on much longer! Most of those worthy folk who advocate reform and lord knows what, have their own axes to grind. My brother Theodore, for instance, wants a bishopric, others want a seat in the Cabinet or a sinecure. Even now I believe there are some who want a peerage, though for the life of me I can't see what good they think it'll do them."

Lord Spratte laughed a little and threw away his cigarette.

"They make a great fuss about redressin' the people's wrongs, but in their heart of hearts I believe they're precious indifferent to them. They want the power which they can cozen out of the mob, or they think the Government will stop their mouths with a fat billet. At first I had an idea you were an impostor like the rest of them, but when you stood up on your hind legs I found out you were nothin' of the kind. You were the only speaker among all those M.P.'s and clerics and millionaires who seemed to mean a word you said. Your speech was quite out of the picture, but it was interesting. Personally I loathe democracy and socialism and all the rest of it, but honest conviction amuses me. To see it on a platform is quite a new sensation."

It made Lord Spratte uncommonly nervous to play the heavy father, and he feared that he was very ridiculous. He waited for Bertram to make an observation.

"I want to do something for my fellows in the few years of my life," said the other, at last.

"You'll find they're much better left alone, and your reward will probably be the most virulent abuse. The human race loves a martyr; it will crucify a man with the greatest zest in order to have another God to worship as soon as the breath is out of his body."

"I'm willing to take the risk," smiled Railing.

"Then in Heaven's name don't hamper yourself by marriage. If you marry out of your own station you'll be nobbled. My boy, before you'd been Winnie's husband twelve months they'd have set you up as a Tory Member of Parliament. On the other hand, if you marry a pauper, you'll have to think of all sorts of shifts to earn bread. You'll have to hold your tongue when you ought to speak, because you daren't risk your means of livelihood."

"I loved Winnie with all my heart and soul."

"I daresay, but you'll get over it. One thinks one's heart is broken and the world is suddenly hollow and empty, but a disappointment in love is like an attack of the gout. It's the very devil while it lasts, but one feels all the better for it afterwards. My dear fellow, I was jilted once. I loved a lady in the Gaiety chorus, and I loved her dearly. But I promise you, not a day passes without my huggin' myself to think I'm still a bachelor."

He gave Bertram his hand, asked him to call soon at his chambers, and jumped into a cab. He was sorry that these efforts at consolation had not been successful, but presently he shrugged his shoulders.

"He'll write a series of articles for a Radical paper on the wickedness of the aristocracy, and that'll soothe him a good sight better than I could."

XIX

CANON SPRATTE was a man of buoyant temper, and did not grieve long over his frustrated hopes. After all there were richer Sees than Barchester. With youth and strength still on his side he need not resign himself yet to insignificance. Importance lay in the position which a man had the ability to make for himself, and the Vicar of St. Gregory's might wield greater power than the bishop of an obscure diocese in the Western provinces. Reconsidering his opinions, he came to the conclusion that Barchester was a dull place, unhealthy, moribund, and tedious. He had always disliked a clay soil. And very soon he sincerely made up his mind that even if it had been offered to him, he would have refused. Like Wilhelm Meister he cried that America was here and now; London offered the only opportunity for such a vigorous character as his. And what were earthly honours to a person of quality?

He consoled himself for everything with the thought that he had steered Winnie successfully through the shoals of her amorous entanglements. She was now staying in the country with Lady Wroxham, and on her return the pleasing news of her engagement would be delivered to an envious world. The Canon flattered himself that her foolish passion for Bertram Railing was definitely extinguished. Her letters to Lady Sophia proved that this facile heart was now given in the properest way to Harry Wroxham. She wrote of him freely, with increasing affection, and her enthusiasm found daily new qualities to admire.

Meanwhile the fine weather gave admirable opportunity for the Canon's matutinal rides with Gwendolen Durant. The effect upon his health was all that could be desired. He found her a more delightful girl than he had ever guessed; and his happy charm quickly brought their acquaintance to such a degree of intimacy that they might have known one another for ten years. It flattered him to see her flashing glance of pleasure when they met each morning, and he exerted himself to entertain her. Sir John also had taken such a fancy to him that much of the Canon's time was spent at the brewer's gorgeous mansion in Park Lane. His urbanity had never been more suave nor the scintillations of his wit more brilliant. Gwendolen hung upon his lips.

But when Canon Spratte thought of Lionel he was a little disconcerted.

On the day Winnie was to come back to London, when he opened his Times at breakfast, the Canon uttered an exclamation. Lady Sophia and Lionel looked up with alarm.

"A dreadful thing has happened," he said, solemnly. "Dr. Gray has had an apoplectic stroke and died last night."

"Poor man," cried Lady Sophia. "He hasn't enjoyed his bishopric long."

"I look upon it as a judgment of Providence," replied her brother, very gravely.

"What on earth do you mean?"

"I said at the time he was not fit to go to Barchester. I have no doubt the excitement and the strain of altering all his plans proved too much for him. You see, I was right. When will men learn to put a rein upon their ambition?"

Canon Spratte read the details carefully, shaking his head, and then turned up the leading articles to see if by chance some reference was made to the sad event. But here a new surprise awaited him. He gave a start and smothered another cry. He ran his eyes down the column quickly to gather its gist, and then perused it with concentrated attention. He forgot entirely that the Church of England had sustained a grievous loss, and that two lamb cutlets on the plate before him sought to tempt his appetite. The news he examined was of vital importance. The brewers, driven beyond endurance, were in full revolt against the Government. On the previous night Sir John Durant, joining in the debate upon the bill to close certain public-houses, had made a violent speech in the House of Commons. The Government's position was insecure already, and if the liquor interest withdrew its support, a dissolution was inevitable. Sir John Durant became suddenly a person of vast importance. The determination he took might throw the money-markets into confusion; it might alter the political balance of Europe and have far-reaching effects in the uttermost parts of the earth. He had paramount influence with the trade and the other members in the House would follow his lead. He could command a large enough number of votes to make Lord Stonehenge's tenure of office impossible. It was certain that the country would not return the Conservative party again. Canon Spratte's heart beat as though he were reading intelligence of the most sensational kind. He threw the paper down and his breath came very fast. For some time he stared straight in front of him and reviewed the situation from every side. He jumped up, and unmindful of his breakfast walked backwards and forwards.

"Aren't you going to eat your chop?" asked Lady Sophia.

"Hang my chop," he cried, impatiently.

She raised her eyebrows.

"How is it possible that the news of Dr. Gray's death can have such an effect on you, Theodore?"

"For goodness' sake be quiet, and let me think," he answered, without his usual politeness.

He had discussed the matter a dozen times with Sir John, and knew with what angry vehemence the brewer regarded this new power wherewith it was proposed to invest the Justices of the Peace. He was a stubborn, obstinate man, and had persuaded himself that it was an interference with the liberty of trade. On the other hand, he was an enthusiastic Conservative, and had no wish to put a Liberal Government in power, which would probably bring in temperance legislation of a much more drastic order. He was filled with the Imperialistic sentiment and dreaded the Radical indifference to his ideal of world supremacy. If Sir John could be induced to hear reason, it was probable that he would not insist on the withdrawal of the bill which public opinion had forced the Government to bring. But if left to himself, he might in a fit of temper throw all his influence with the Opposition. Whoever had Durant's ear on this occasion was for the moment the most powerful man in England. A smile broke on the Canon's lips. He drew a long breath.

"Sophia, I should like to speak a few words to Lionel."

"I've just finished," she said.

She did not hurry herself, but when it pleased her left the room. Canon Spratte turned eagerly to his son.

"Now, Lionel, I think you've shilly-shallied long enough. I want to know for good and all what you propose to do with regard to Gwendolen."

"What do you mean, father?"

"Good lord, man, you're not a perfect fool, are you? We've discussed your marriage ad nauseam. I want to know what your intentions are. It's not fair to the girl to keep her dangling in this fashion. Are you going to marry her or not?"

"Well, father, there's no hurry about it?"

"On the contrary there's the greatest possible hurry."

"Why?"

"I have every reason to believe that some one else is thinking of proposing to her."

"Well, I don't think she cares twopence about me," answered Lionel, rather sulkily. "Lately when I've seen her she's talked of nothing but you."

"There are less diverting topics of conversation, Lionel," retorted the Canon, with a smile.

"One can have too much of a good thing."

"If you don't look sharp some one else will step in and cut you out. I warn you candidly."

"I shan't break my heart, father."

Canon Spratte shrugged his shoulders.

"I don't know what the young men of the present day are coming to; they have no spirit and no enterprise. Anyhow, I've done my duty and you mustn't be surprised whatever happens."

"I wonder you don't marry her yourself," said Lionel, ironically.

"And would you have anything to say against my doing so?" retorted the Canon, not without a suspicion of temper. "Let me tell you that a man of fifty is in the very flower of his age. I flatter myself there are few men of your years who have half the vigour and energy that I have."

He flung out of the room in a huff. His horse had been waiting for half-an-hour, and it was later than usual when he joined Gwendolen in the Park. Her face lit up, and from his own all sign of vexation had vanished.

"I'd given you up," she said. "I thought you weren't able to come."

"Would you have been disappointed if I hadn't?"

"Awfully!"

"You make me regret more than ever that I'm not twenty-five," he said, without any beating about the bush.

"Why?"

"Because if I were I should promptly ask you to marry me."

"If you were I should probably refuse you," she smiled.

"I wonder what you mean by that?"

They walked their horses side by side, and the Canon was seized with an unaccountable shyness. It was by a real effort of will that at last he forced himself to speak.

"I suppose it never struck you that I took more than common pleasure in our conversations. But when I left you I was always seized with despair. I realized that my heart had remained as young as ever it was, but you never ceased to see in me a man old enough to be your father. Do you know that I'm fifty?"

"I never asked myself what your age was. I never felt that you were any older than I."

She answered nervously, looking straight in front of her. The Canon shot a sidelong glance in her direction and saw that her cheeks were flaming. He recovered his courage at once. Faint heart, he knew, never won fair lady.

"Gwendolen, I sometimes think that you have worked a miracle, for by your side I feel as young as the summer morning. What can the years matter when I have the spirit and the strength of a youth! I admire you and I love you. Do you think me very ridiculous?"

She shook her head, but did not speak. He put his hand lightly on hers.

"Gwendolen, will you be my wife?"

She looked up with a little laugh that was almost hysterical. She did not answer directly.

"I'll race you to the end," she said.

Without a word, smiling, the Canon put the spurs to his horse; and they galloped up the Row at a speed which was altogether beyond reason. The policeman on his beat watched with gaping mouth the strange spectacle of a comely young woman and an ecclesiastical dignitary, no longer in his first youth but handsome too, peltering towards the Achilles Statue as fast as they could go. Gwendolen's horse kept somewhat ahead, but the Canon would not give way. Again he clapped his spurs to the straining flanks. It seemed to him, romantically, that he rode for a great prize, and in his excitement he could have shouted at the top of his voice. They reached the end neck and neck, and when they stopped, panting, the horses were white with lather. There was no longer a shadow of humility in the Canon's breezy manner.

"And now for my answer," he cried, gaily.

"What about Lionel?" she smiled, blushing.

"Oh, Lionel can go to the dickens."

Canon Spratte frequently said that he was unaccustomed to let grass grow under his feet. Having left Gwendolen at the door, he returned to the Vicarage, changed his clothes, and promptly took a cab back to Park Lane. But he found that she had been before him, and Sir John Durant was already in possession of the happy news.

"Upon my soul, I don't know what you've done to the girl," he said, in his hearty, boisterous tone. "She's quite infatuated."

The Canon laughed and rubbed his hands.

"She's made me the happiest of men."

Sir John was a man of affairs, whose pride it was that he went straight to the point; and notwithstanding Canon Spratte's remonstrance, who sought to waive the matter airily aside, he insisted on discussing at once the business part of the projected union. It required all the fortunate lover's self-control to prevent a little gasp of pleased surprise when the brewer in a casual way mentioned the sum he proposed to settle on his only daughter. It was larger even than he had expected.

"My dear Durant, your generosity overwhelms me," he cried. "I promise you I will do my best to make her happy, and I think it's unlikely that either my brother or Lionel will ever marry. In all probability Gwendolen's eldest son will inherit the title."

This settled, he turned deftly to the political situation, and discovered that the brewer was somewhat taken aback by the responsibility which appeared to have fallen on him. He was anxious to do his duty by his party, but at the same time could not bear to sacrifice the interests of his trade. He had come to no decision whatever, and showed himself only too pleased to discuss his predicament with a man whose experience was so large, and whose mind so lucid. He insisted that his prospective son-in-law should stay to luncheon. During this meal Canon Spratte proved very neatly his skill in social intercourse, for he was able to show himself gallant and tender towards Gwendolen, while at the same time he displayed keen sympathy with the brewer's perplexity. But no sooner was the meal over than he jumped to his feet.

"You're not going already?" cried Sir John.

"My dear fellow, I must. I have a very busy day before me." He smiled tenderly at Gwendolen. "You can imagine that it is not without weighty reasons that I tear myself away."

"Then you must come back to dinner. You know, it's private members' night and I'm not going to the House."

"Impossible also! Winnie is returning from the country to-day, and it would be unkind if I did not dine at home. Besides, I have asked my brother. A Christian family is one of the most beautiful as it is one of the most characteristic sights of our English life. I like to allow its mellowing influence to be exerted as often as possible on my rather harum-scarum relative."

"Then when shall we see you again?" asked the brewer, firmly grasping his hand.

"If it won't disturb you I should like to come in for half-an-hour about ten o'clock."

As soon as the door was closed behind him, he hailed a passing cab.

"I'll give you a florin if you can get to the Athenæum in three minutes," he cried to the driver. He looked at his watch. "I think I shall just catch him."

He knew that Lord Stonehenge was in the habit of passing an hour at the Athenæum after luncheon. He sat always in a certain chair, near the window, which by common consent was invariably left vacant for him. No one ventured to disturb him. He went in and out of the club, indifferent to his fellow-members, as if he did not notice that a soul was there. But Canon Spratte was an audacious man and did not fear to be importunate. He smiled with satisfaction when he saw Lord Stonehenge, heavily seated in his accustomed place. That vast mass of flesh had a ponderous immobility which suggested that it would be difficult for the Prime Minister to escape from his agile hands. He was turning over the pages of a review, but his mind appeared busy with other things.

Canon Spratte walked up jauntily with the Westminster Gazette in his hand. It contained a very amusing cartoon in which Sir John Durant, as a Turkish pasha, was seated on a beer-barrel, while the Prime Minister, in the garb of an odalisque, knelt humbly before him with uplifted hands. In the background were two satellites, one with a bow-string and the other with a scimitar.

"Have you seen this?" said the Canon, sitting down coolly and handing the paper. "Capital, isn't it?"

The Prime Minister turned his listless eyes on the intruder and for a moment wondered who on earth he was.

"I've just been lunching with Durant. He's rather sore about it. Ticklish situation, isn't it?"

"Are you Theodore Spratte?" asked Lord Stonehenge.

"I am," laughed the Canon. "I hope Durant won't do anything rash. I have a good deal of influence with him, and of course I'm doing my best to persuade him not to kick over the traces."

A sudden light flashed in the Prime Minister's eyes, and he saw that Canon Spratte had an object in thus speaking to him. He dived into the abysses of his memory, and recalled that he had offered him a deanery, which the Canon had refused. The man evidently wanted a bishopric or nothing. He remembered also something that his daughter had told him; he wondered what power the suave parson actually had with Sir John.

"I hear that your son is going to marry Durant's daughter," he said, slowly.

"You've been misinformed," answered the Canon, with a smile that was somewhat ironical. "I am going to marry her."

"You!"

They looked at one another like two fencers, seeking to discover their strength in each other's face. The Prime Minister's eyes had a peculiar force which suggested the reason of his long-continued power; they lacked brilliancy, but there was in them a curious intensity of vision which seemed to absorb the thoughts of other men's minds. The silence lasted interminably. Canon Spratte bore the great man's gaze with perfect steadfastness, and presently Lord Stonehenge looked away. He stared out of the window, into space, and the Canon thought he had entirely forgotten the subject in hand.

"I need not tell you that I will do everything I can to bring Durant to a reasonable state of mind. At present he's wavering. You probably know the facts better than I do, but he tells me the liquor party will follow him. I understand if they go against you the result will be—awkward."

Lord Stonehenge apparently did not hear. His eyes still rested heavily on the trees in the park. Canon Spratte began to grow a little irritated, but still he waited patiently. At last the Prime Minister spoke.

"I suppose you've heard that Gray is dead?"

"I have."

"Would you like to go to Barchester?"

Although he seemed desperately stupid Lord Stonehenge had understood. The Canon's heart gave a leap and he caught his breath. He forgot that Barchester stood on a clay soil, and it no longer seemed a tedious place. At last! But he showed no eagerness to accept. He knew as well as the Prime Minister that the Government was in the hollow of his hand.

At that moment a bishop came up to Lord Stonehenge with a telegram in his hand. Canon Spratte gave him an impatient frown.

"I'm sorry to disturb you, but I think you ought to see this," said the newcomer.

He handed the telegram to Lord Stonehenge, who glanced at it irritably. The bishop knew Canon Spratte and nodded to him.

"It's to tell me that the Bishop of Sheffield died in his sleep early this morning. He's been ailing for some time."

"Thank you," said the Prime Minister.

He returned the telegram, and the bishop withdrew. Canon Spratte and Lord Stonehenge looked at one another once more. A new factor had come into the game which they were playing. Beside Sheffield the diocese of Barchester was quite insignificant; it was small and poor, and from the city itself all prosperity had long since vanished. The bishop of such a place might be a great man in his own neighbourhood, but he had no chance of activity outside it. Sheffield, on the other hand, possessed two suffragans and patronage of vast importance. It was the centre of religious life in the Midlands. Year by year the town was growing in consequence; and its bishop, if a man of resource, might wield great power. By help of the rich manufacturers in his district he could raise huge sums for any purpose he pleased, and his influence need be second only to that of the archbishop. If it was possible to have Sheffield, Barchester was but a poor reward for such services as Theodore Spratte could render to his country. But he had no time to think it over. It was necessary to make his decision there and then. He was a bold man and did not hesitate.

Lord Stonehenge still waited for his answer.

"It's very good of you to make me such an offer, and I need not say I am grateful for the honour, but—if I may put it frankly—I don't think I feel inclined to go to such a dead and alive town as Barchester. I have a passion for work, and I can't live without plenty to do. If I leave London at all it must be for a place that offers ample scope for a man of energy, a place where there's a vigorous civic life, and where you may feel yourself, as it were, at the centre of this busy modern world of ours. Advance and progress are my watchwords."

Conversation with Lord Stonehenge was difficult, for he seldom opened his mouth. When you had said what you wanted, he merely waited for you to begin again; and unless possessed of much effrontery, you were utterly disconcerted. In the present case, however, there was but one word he needed to utter, and that word was Sheffield. It remained unspoken. Canon Spratte, content to let things take their time, got up.

"But it's too bad of me to take up the only moment in the day you have for recreation. I shall be seeing Durant again after dinner."

With a nod and a smile he left the Prime Minister to his own reflections.

Theodore's day had been somewhat exhausting. It is given to few, however eagerly they pursue the art of life, within twelve hours to win a wife and to refuse a bishopric. He had thoroughly earned the bath he took before dinner. He wondered how many people knew that he, Theodore Spratte, then pleasantly wallowing in cold water, mother naked, held as in a balance the destinies of the British Empire. Sir John Durant would do as he suggested, and the next few hours might see determined the fall of an administration. He rubbed himself joyously with rough towels.

"When the Clergy and the Licensed Victualers stand shoulder to shoulder, not all the powers of Satan can avail against them," he cried.

He dressed with unusual care and shaved a second time; he brushed his hair with feminine nicety. He put two rings on his little finger, and with a sigh of complete satisfaction, looked at himself in the glass. He felt very well and young and happy. His appetite was good and he was prepared to enjoy an excellent dinner.

When he reached the drawing-room he found that Lord Spratte was already arrived. Winnie, whom he had not seen since her return, came up to kiss him.

"Well, my dear, I hope you enjoyed yourself. You look positively radiant."

"I'm so happy, father. You don't know what a dear Harry is. I'm awfully grateful to you."

"Your father's a wise man, darling," he laughed.

Lionel came in, hat in hand, to see Winnie, who had arrived but half-an-hour before and gone straight to her room. He expressed his regret that a choir-practice, which he must attend, forced him to go out.

"Well, my boy, I'm sorry you can't dine with us," said the Canon. "I should have liked to see my family united round my table on this night of all others, but since your duty calls I have no more to say."

At this moment Ponsonby announced that dinner was served, and at the same time handed a telegram to his master.

"Hulloa, what's this?"

He opened it and gave a cry. His heart beat so violently that he was obliged to sit down.

"Papa, what's the matter?" cried Winnie.

"It's so stupid of me, I'm quite upset. Get me a glass of sherry, Ponsonby."

"What is it, Theodore?" asked Lady Sophia, anxiously.

He waved his family aside and would not speak till Ponsonby brought the wine. He drank a glass of sherry. A sigh of relief issued from his lips. He waited till Ponsonby had left the room, and then slowly rose to his feet.

"Sophia, you will be gratified to learn that the Government has offered me the vacant bishopric of Sheffield."

"Oh, papa, I'm so glad," said Winnie.

Lionel seized his father's hand and wrung it warmly.

"Well, Sophia, what do you say?"

"Presumably you don't want me to persuade you to take it."

"No, I shall accept as it is offered me, frankly—and by telegram."

He looked upon the members of his family and took no pains to hide his intense satisfaction.

"But I'm keeping you from your duties, Lionel. You mustn't wait a moment longer." His son went to the door, but the Canon called him back. “One moment, I was forgetting. I think the time has now arrived to announce Winnie’s betrothal publicly. Just sit down and write out a notice; you can leave it at the News Agency as you pass.”

Lionel obediently went to the desk and took a pen. The Canon cleared his throat.

“We are authorized to announce that a marriage has been arranged between Lord Wroxham, of Castle Tanker, and Winifred, only daughter of the Honourable, (write that in full, Lionel,) of the Honourable and Reverend Canon Theodore Spratte, bishop elect of Sheffield; better known as the——”

“Better known as the—yes?”

“You’re very dull, Lionel,” exclaimed the Canon, with a laugh that was somewhat irritable. “Better known as the popular and brilliant Vicar of St. Gregory’s, South Kensington.”

When Lionel had departed with this, Canon Spratte turned jovially to his brother.

“Well, Thomas, you see that virtue is sometimes rewarded even in this world. It is a great blessing to me to think that everything I desired has come about. Winnie is to marry a man who will make her an excellent husband, and she will occupy a position which she cannot fail to adorn. While as for myself I am removing to a sphere where such poor abilities as Providence has endowed me with, will have a fuller scope. I confess that I am gratified, not only for myself, but for the honour which has befallen our house. I cannot help regretting that my dear father is not alive to see this day. I need not say, Thomas, that I shall always be pleased to see you at Sheffield. I am convinced that the golf-links are excellent, and the poor hospitality of the Palace will ever be at the command of the head of my family.”

“Theodore, I shouldn’t like to be a rebellious parson in your diocese,” said Lord Spratte, gravely. “You’ll make it very hot for any one who don’t act accordin’ to your lights.”

“I shall not forget the watchwords of our house, which have ever been Advance and Progress. To these I shall now add: ‘Discipline.’ But really we should go down to dinner.”

Lady Sophia thought it high time, for she had a healthy appetite. But at that instant came another interruption. Ponsonby entered the room.

“A gentleman wishes to see you, sir,” he said, handing a card to the Canon.

“Oh, I can see no one at this hour. I can’t keep dinner waiting a moment longer.”

"I told him you could see nobody, sir," answered Ponsonby, "but the gentleman said he came from the Daily Mail."

"That certainly makes a difference," said the Canon, taking the card.

"That's what I thought, sir. He said he would be very much obliged if you could grant him a short interview."

"Say I shall be very happy, Ponsonby, and show him into my study."

"Theodore, are we to have no dinner?" cried Lady Sophia, when Ponsonby was gone.

"Dinner, dinner!" exclaimed Canon Spratte, scornfully. "How can I think of dinner now, Sophia? I have a duty to perform. You forgot that my position is radically altered."

"I knew you'd remind us of it in less than five minutes," said Lady Sophia, who felt that firmness now was needed or the future would be unbearable.

"I and my family have always been in the vanguard of progress," replied the bishop elect, with a glance at the Lord Chancellor's portrait.

"I know, but even your family wants its dinner sometimes."

"Sophia, I shall be obliged if you will not interrupt me. I cannot say I think it kind of you to insist in this vulgar way on the satisfaction of a gross and sensual appetite. I should have thought on such an occasion worthier thoughts would occupy your mind. But if your flesh is weak I am willing that you should begin. I am not a selfish man, and Heaven forbid that I should ask as a right what an affectionate and Christian disposition should grant as a pleasure."

"Fiddlesticks!"

Canon Spratte looked his sister up and down. He held himself very erect.

"Sophia, I have long felt that you do not treat me with the respect I venture to consider my due. I must really beg you not to act towards me any longer with this mixture of indecent frivolity and vulgar cynicism. I do not wish to remind you that there is a change in my position."

"You have done so twice in five minutes," said Lady Sophia, acidly.

"It appears to be necessary. Once for all, however, let me inform you that henceforth I expect to be treated in a different fashion. If you have not the affection to respect your brother Theodore, if you have not the delicacy of sentiment to respect the son of the late Lord Chancellor—you will at least respect the Bishop of Sheffield."

He stood for a moment to allow the effect of his words to be duly felt, and then marched to the door. Here he stopped and turned round.

"It may also interest you to learn that on the thirty-first of July I am going to be married to Gwendolen Durant."

He went out and slammed the door behind him. Lady Sophia stared at her eldest brother with helpless astonishment; but with a little smile, Lord Spratte shrugged his shoulders.

"He always has had the last word, Sophia."

XX

The Times of the third of May in the following year contained the subjoined announcement:

SPRATTE. On the 1st instant, at the Palace, the wife of the Right Revd. the Bishop of Sheffield, (the Honourable Theodore Spratte,) of a son.

Richard Clay & Sons, Limited, London and Bungay.